WELCOME TO MORMYR

The sky seemed to be about twenty feet above our heads, a boiling curtain of vapors that writhed from blue to grey to red. All the colors were very dark—though it was daylight here there was less light to see by than the stars provided at night elsewhere—and they gave the impression of being spectral patterns in an oil-slick. I have never seen a sky which gave the impression of being so heavy. It was not merely oppressive, it was positively claustrophobic. It was as though the ground was one surface and the clouds another, with the merest crack between them. And it was all too easy to conjure up the impression that the crack was slowly closing, the sky slowly falling.

And the sky was angry . . .

And so were the passengers in this death trip along the bottom surface of a vicious gas giant—for their captain was a madman and their destination a vengeful delusion. . . .

THE
FENRIS
DEVICE

Brian M. Stableford

DAW BOOKS, INC.
DONALD A. WOLLHEIM, PUBLISHER

1301 Avenue of the Americas
New York, N. Y.   10019

DEDICATION:

For Crad and Wendy Owen

FIRST PRINTING, DECEMBER 1974

1 2 3 4 5 6 7 8 9

PRINTED IN U.S.A.

1

I'm a spaceman. I like space. I like flying space, and I know every trick that makes it easier, every trick which enables me to cope with the eccentricities of space better than the next man. I feel at home in deep space and I can handle virtually anything which deep space is disposed to throw at me. Handling the *Hooded Swan* in deep space was a joy and a privilege.

But the *Hooded Swan*, so its architect declared, was a good deal more versatile than an honest spaceship. It was not his purpose, he said, to use the *Swan* merely as a means of transporting him from point A to point B—a job which could be done almost as well by any common-or-garden p-shifter. He had always intended that the *Hooded Swan* should do things which no other ship in existence was capable of doing. That was why he had hired me. Well, things hadn't worked out quite as he'd planned, because he was a very busy man, and he'd found other employment for both the *Swan* and myself which was (he said) not very demanding.

And so, he said, when the opportunity arose to further his fondest dreams and—at one and the same time—to use the *Hooded Swan* in an environment for which no other spaceship in the galaxy was fitted, he was highly delighted.

I was not. Quite the reverse, in fact.

I hate atmosphere. While recognizing that certain kinds of atmosphere are not only useful but highly desirable in that they are necessary to life—specifically my life—I feel that atmosphere is no place for a self-respecting spaceman to be piloting a self-respecting spacecraft.

And when "atmosphere" is a euphemism for a cloud-filled, storm-torn inferno such as one finds on a world like Leucifer V, then I feel absolutely justified in feeling nothing less than hatred for it.

I don't doubt that the *Swan* was equipped to deal with it. Charlot certainly didn't doubt it, because he was on board, peering over my shoulder, and he was presumably a better judge than I of *theoretical* capabilities. I'm a practical man, and I'm ready enough to admit that it was I, not the ship, who was inadequate to the task. But Charlot didn't accept excuses of that kind. Charlot was a man who believed in theoretical capabilities. He made no concessions to human weakness.

I dipped into the atmosphere feeling very much like the proverbial snowflake in hell. I was traveling at mere thousands of kph, and slowing still, preparing to use the wings to get lift. I would get the lift anyway, and I figured it was far better to try to use it—absorb it into my system—than to fight it with the cannons and the flux. I wished that I could screw my ship-body up into a tight sphere, fall like a cannonball through a couple of thousand kilometers of atmosphere, and then miraculously unfurl and take instant control of myself just above the ground. But the ground was a difficult thing to find on Leucifer V. It hid beneath a cloak of tidal, flying dust, whipped up by perpetual blizzards. Even if I were capable of masquerading as a falling stone, there could be no easy way down. I couldn't "unfurl" in conditions like that—I'd be ripped apart. No, I had to go down slowly, with my wings spread and my effective mass denatured as far as I dared, pretending to be an autumn leaf rather than a creature of steel and flesh.

As the atmosphere closed in around me my ship-senses

gave me a sudden, irrational claustrophobia, a sensation of drowning, of being smothered by soft cloth. I shook it off.

I drifted on a long decaying arc, just accepting the effects of the thickening air into the balanced flux-cycle. I filled the cortex of the driver with as much power as it would hold, knowing that I would need all I could get. Slowly, I began to drain the shields. At the kind of velocity I was making now they'd be far more of a hindrance than a help. No matter how streamlined a ship is, even a ship with a manipulable skin like the *Swan*, there is absolutely no way of evening out matter-scarring in the shields. And down below I'd have far too much on my plate to want to bother with eddy currents in the shields. If a seized shield immobilized one of my limbs for even a second it could be fatal. On the other hand, as I stripped the shields I became more and more aware of the atmosphere tearing at my skin, burning me, pecking and clawing at me. The farther I went down, the sharper the blades that would cut at me. I knew I was going to bleed, ship-body and cradle-body both, and I was going to hurt and hurt bad.

"Ready," I said to Eve. She was standing beside me, with the medical kit ready. We'd already worked out the sorts of shots I was liable to need, and a code by which I could call for them. She had to needle the first shot into me—I wasn't rigged for an intravenous feed because I didn't want equipment attached to me blurring the sensations I was getting from the outer skin. Painful those sensations might be, but on my correct reading of them and compensating for them would depend the life of the ship.

"Johnny," I said, as we dropped deeper and deeper.

"Waiting," he said. "Nothing yet."

I had to keep the relaxation web over .9 in order to keep our effective mass as close to zero as was desirable, and when the web is so tight the deration system is at its most sensitive. An imbalance of any kind at the discharge points would cause the flux to bleed. Some bleeding would be virtually inevitable, but we would have to keep the loss under control. And "we" meant not just me, but Johnny too. This was going to be tough for him—by far and away his toughest yet.

How are you? I asked the wind.

—All set, he told me.

There were long seconds of silence while nothing happened. I continued to thin out the shields with careful slowness, feeling like a striptease dancer at rehearsal. There was an awkward phase when the sensation of the air molecules flickering over my skin was like an itch or an insistent tickle, but I knew that of old, and it didn't bother me. We were through the phase quickly, and I began to feel the steady, prickling pressure build up. I've never worn a hair shirt, but I imagine it might be something like that. The deeper we went the heavier the pressure, but that wasn't the worst of it. As we plunged deeper and deeper, the turbulence began to build up around us. The *Swan* was designed to compensate for turbulence— she had wings like a bird, nerves and motors which could make all kinds of changes in her outer skin to give her total dynamic streamlining. But nothing's perfect, and there was always something I couldn't cancel. It was like groping fingers sliding over me, sometimes light, sometimes clumsy.

Inside the control room, everything was steady as a rock. It all looked easy from the back seat, and the time that dragged by made things worse, not better, for the people watching me. They had no way of understanding, no way of feeling what I was feeling, no way of sensing the disaster that was lurking in the corners of my eyes. For them, it was just like grooving in total vacuum, save that I was radiating tension and concentration.

As the shields faded into gossamer, the whole subsurface came alive and alert.

"Give me the second now," I said, amazed by the calmness of my voice.

I felt the anesthetic slide home into my arm, and almost automatically my brain began to count off the seconds to densensitivity.

The relief seemed to last for only a few seconds. The

insistence of the atmosphere overrode the numbing effect and the subsurface still felt sore and reactive.

—Don't take any more, warned the wind, or I'll lose my control.

OK, I said, soothing him.

I had no intention of knocking either of us out.

Within a couple of minutes more, we began to find clouds, and things were suddenly dramatically changed.

"Here we go," I said, aiming the comment at Johnny.

The pain took me across the back, first, like a muscle cramp. We were slow now—no more than a few hundred kph, but the slower we went the harder it was to balance the flux to the nth decimal. The web felt virtually nonexistent, and the whole drive-unit felt like putty inside me. I felt half dead, and yet I had to move with the grace of an eagle and the delicacy of a hummingbird. I felt the anesthetic that was calming my body begin to swim up around my brain.

"Stim," I said.

The needle slid home again. I knew—and so did Eve—that hyping up on the drugs at the rate I was doing could only have a bad effect in the end, but I had to buy all the temporary help I could, and if I suffered tomorrow . . . well, at least I was alive to suffer. I don't like being shot up any more than the next man, but I'm not proud. I don't court disaster. No doubt, in the final analysis, it would take years off my life, but when you weigh the odds . . .

"Watch it," said Johnny.

He didn't need to. I could feel the flux slipping like sand between my fingers. I could feel the danger floating up around me, like a wave of nausea. I felt my face muscles contract as I wrestled with the controls. I could feel Johnny's hands somewhere inside me, working away at the driver, milking the cortex, using his hands and his delicate touch as he'd never been called upon to do in his life. The flux cycled. We didn't bleed. We had her under control.

And still we went down, angling deep into the atmosphere of Leucifer V, the world the Gallacellans called Mormyr, and still the drop seemed limitless, and the sensors could pick up nothing down below but an abyss filled with storms. I took thrust out of the drivers, feeding it through the flux and into the cortex, restoring the reserve and reducing our forward impulse so that we fell steeper and steeper. Still I felt sore, but the pain was under control. The drugs and the wind between them were keeping me up to the job. So far, so good.

But it could only get worse.

The double sensation began to trouble me. I could feel the ghosts of Eve and Titus Charlot hovering over me in the atmosphere of the planet, like demons following the ship on its descent, watching her like hawks, urging her on faster . . . to her doom?

I felt the flux struggling. It really was *trying* to stay with me, to help me, but it was being scourged by the winds and the vapors that were howling around the ship. I could feel the *Swan* giving me all she could, trying her level best to do it on her own, without the pilot inheriting her suffering and her peril. I poured myself into the bird's synapses, we merged totally, and I was embodied in the flux that held strong against the torture, sheltered neither by the shields nor by the relaxation web to any degree. It was like a spider walking through the chambers of my heart, like centipedes moving in my bloodstream, like a great fireworm writhing slowly in my gut. I felt myself begin to open up inside, ever so slowly, ever so gently, without pain, without the raggedness of tearing, and I felt myself begin to spill out within myself.

And lower and lower we came, into the clouds of black dust and ice, into the rage of the storm which whirled and stabbed at us. I was bleeding. I was losing flux. I could feel Johnny working away, with all the speed he could muster, all the fineness of feeling. He had the touch, there was no doubt. He was good, but he wasn't good enough. I opened up wider and wider inside myself, and I bled.

The sensors told me at last that there was a down to go

to, that there was a bottom to the gravity pit, that there was a haven if only I could reach it, but it was too late. Johnny was losing and Johnny was panicking. I could feel it rising inside him as it flooded into the movements of his fingers that were inside me. I could feel the flux giving way to his hysteria and the mad insistency of the storm.

I could feel myself—and it was almost with surprise that I did so—being racked with hideous, *squeezing* pain, and I knew that there was nothing I could do but run. I tried to cry out, hoping that even a wordless cry might stabilize Johnny, might tell Eve that I needed another boost, might even tell Charlot that what he wanted me to do simply could not be done. But I could manage no cry. My jaw was locked, and the only one who knew was the wind, locked inside with me, in rigid agony.

The last vestiges of power were flooding from the cortex into the deration system. The flux was jammed. I discharged the cannons to shock the whole unit into some imitation of life, and I blasted power through the nervenet of the ship. With a single convulsive maneuver—something no bird, no spaceship, no other thing in the galaxy except the *Hooded Swan* and I could have done—I began to throw a surge of strength into the web.

The flux stirred, and with it Johnny. We fought, all of us—*Swan,* Johnny, the wind, and I—and we found enough to turn us, enough to give us the power to jump. Just enough to run away. Full flight, in full terror. From somewhere, we managed to make some kind of a syndrome, and we were up and away as the flux fed on herself.

The pain really took me then as we went up. No shield at all, nothing to protect me. I felt as though I were burning alive, my skin blistering and and bubbling and turning to black, cold dust on my bones.

But the *Swan* was equal even to that. Johnny built the syndrome—Johnny and the wind—and they found power for the driver, power for the cannons, and—at last—power for the shields. Up and up we soared, and I realized that we were all of us alive, and would stay that way.

I managed sound . . . I think it was the word "Go."

And go we did. We climbed in seconds what it had taken us long minutes to fall. We cleared, we found space again. Still I was rigid in the cradle, my body and my agony dissipated throughout the ship, still fighting for every last vestige of power the syndrome could provide. All of us, we were united in those dragging seconds, all in a single purpose.

And we made it.

By the time we found space, I was absolutely helpless in the cradle, with no more involvement with my tiny, human self than an unborn child. Even as we headed deep into the system-vacuum, I had only one sensation that I could relate to my bodily self alone, rather than to my total, participant ship-self, and that was a sensation of leakage. My bladder had emptied, and there was blood running from both corners of my mouth to mingle with my tears.

Eve was mopping me up. As consciousness returned to its habitual mode of residence, I could feel her wet cloth stroking back and forth across my face. I could hear Charlot breathing.

There were long minutes of waiting, when nobody dared say a word. Not to anyone, about anything. The two Gallacellans who waited in the rear of the control room were absolutely impassive, waiting. Nick delArco had nothing to say.

Inevitably, it was Charlot who broke the silence.

"Less than a hundred meters," he said. That was all. Just: *Less than a hundred meters*. No sympathy, no understanding. All he was interested in was how close we had come before we had failed. He *knew* that if we could get down to the last kilometer—to one-tenth of the last kilometer—then it was *theoretically* possible for us to have gone the whole way. He just didn't see the blood that was coming out of me. All he saw was that we had come within seconds of victory, and had failed.

"It's impossible," I said. "It can't be done."

"You were there," he said. "You were there but for a matter of meters."

"It makes no difference," I said. "A meter or a parsec. Those last hundred meters were the worst of all. Nothing could live in that. Nothing. There's no way down through those last hundred meters. No way."

"You had power left," he said. "Power to run away."

"And if I'd used that power to go down?" I said, my voice hoarse as the flow of the argument matched the flow of feeling coming back into my body—and with the feeling, renewed pain. "What would I have used to come away?" I finished.

"Once we were down . . ." he began.

"And what if we ran out with ten meters still to go?" I interrupted. "Or ten centimeters? All we had to do was roll over . . . and we'd be down forever."

"It was my fault," Johnny's voice came over the circuit. "It was my fault. If I could have held the flux just a few seconds . . . I lost her. It wasn't Grainger's fault. . . ."

Of all the help I'd never needed . . .

"Is that true?" said Charlot.

"Nobody could have held it," I said. "Nobody. Johnny was brilliant. Nobody could have done more. Not Rothgar, not Jesus Christ. Nobody human can land a ship on that world. It just cannot be done."

"I could have done it," said Johnny, his voice sounding like the knell of doom. "If only . . ."

"Will you shut your bloody mouth!" I howled at him. "You want to go down there again? Don't be a fool. You did your best. Your ultimate best. There's no more that could be done. It's impossible. There's no point in whining, now or ever. You have to realize that there are some things that just can't be done."

—It can be done, said the wind, and you know it.

I didn't need him. Yes, it could be done, with a perfect engineer and a perfect pilot. The ship could do it. But Johnny was only Johnny, and I wasn't making any claims for myself. Yes, it could be done. But only by a lunatic. And only a lunatic would suggest to Charlot that there was any point at all in making another attempt. He was only human. He couldn't send us down again. Not if there was no way.

Stylaster—the Gallacellan for whose bennefit all this pantomime had been staged—said something in his native tongue. No human knew the language—the Gallacellans guarded their privacy—so we all had to wait for the interpreter. His name was Ecdyon.

"Stylaster says that your pilot has been damaged," said Ecdyon, addressing Charlot. "Will he have to be replaced for the second attempt?"

I gave him the filthiest look I could conjure up. It was wasted. What can a filthy look mean to an alien? Ecdyon knew the score, and I was willing to bet that Stylaster knew as well. They were playing a tough game. This was a real test for Charlot's famed diplomatic talents.

"The pilot cannot be replaced," said Charlot, speaking to Ecdyon but keeping one eye on me. "He will have to be rested until he is well. Then we will talk about a second attempt."

"You can talk all you bloody well like," I said. "But I'm not going back down there again."

"We'll talk about it later," said Charlot, ominously, and quietly, because Ecdyon was busy clicking away at Stylaster in Gallacellan.

"It's impossible," I said.

"That's for me to decide."

"Like hell it is," I said. "You only own this ship. I fly it and Nick is the captain. The only man who can order me to fly back into that hell is Captain delArco. Now *he* knows I'm serious when I say it can't be done, and *he*'s not going to order me to do it. So legally, Mr. Charlot, you can't touch me."

He looked at me with pure poison in his gaze. All the politeness and the helpfulness and the almost-friendship that we'd built up on Pharos was gone. He was an old man. He was a sick man. If there was one thing he wanted to do more than any other before he died it was to make meaningful contact with the Gallacellans. In the five centuries since the Gallacellans met the human race on Leucifer IV there had been exactly one opportunity to make that contact, and this was it. Only Grainger and the bounds of possibility stood between Charlot and Stylaster, and Charlot was not the man to respect the bounds of possibility. So what chance had Grainger?

"Captain delArco will follow my instructions," said Charlot coldly, getting angrier by the minute because he knew that every word would get back to Stylaster, now or later.

"Captain delArco had better think long and hard about that," I said. "And so had you. Because between you and me and anyone else who can hear me, I won't take this ship back down into the atmosphere of that planet. You can have me thrown in jail till I rot, between you, if you have a mind to. But any other attempt at landing on Mormyr is an attempt at suicide and murder, and I won't do it."

I had to put my case across in the strongest possible terms. It was no good at all saying "It's too dangerous" or "I'm scared" or "It hurts." Nothing short of impossibility was going to stop Charlot, so impossibility was what he was going to get. I'd gone in once, because I had no way to refuse. But I wasn't going back. In my humble opinion, no one had the right to ask that of me. And privately, I had every confidence that when it came to the crunch, Nick delArco wasn't going to be Charlot's puppet.

"You *have* to try again," said Charlot.

"No," said Eve, who was still waiting for the blood to stop oozing from my mouth. "He can't. He's right. It would kill him."

I was really and truly thankful to have that support just then. Johnny had the sense to keep his mouth shut, and Nick delArco had absolutely nothing to say—yet.

I reached out to take the controls in my hands again, and Eve slipped the hood back down over my eyes. We were just drifting in a loose orbit around Leucifer, heading away from Mormyr.

"Shall we go home?" I asked.

"We'll go back to Iniomi," said Charlot. "We'll get you back into shape. Then we can discuss what to do next."

I began to set us on a course for the fourth world.

Stylaster clicked for a moment or two, like a demented typewriter.

"Stylaster says," Ecdyon translated, "that your ship was most impressive. He is very confident that we will be successful."

"Bastard," I muttered, not loudly enough for the interpreter to hear. A moment later, I regretted not saying it louder, so that Ecdyon could have passed it on. But it was too late to repeat it.

—I still think . . . began the wind.

I know, I said. Shut up.

Then I slipped the *Swan* into the groove.

2

Once we were down on Iniomi I was fit for nothing except crawling into my bunk and waiting for the doctor. I didn't want to do that and I had no intention of doing anything that I didn't want to do right at that moment. So I dumped the ship in the yard like a sack of potatoes and I dragged my tired frame out of her belly, and I went walking in the alien night.

The stars were bright, and they were packed closer than I usually see them in the skies of the worlds where I habitually make my living. Brighter even than the stars of New Alexandria. Leucifer was close to the core—some even called her a core star. But we—the human race—hadn't touched the *real* core stars. That was bad space to fly, and the worlds were bad, too. We stayed away, in the regions which were more fitting for our kind of people. Perhaps we would have gone farther into the core, extended the tentacles of interstellar human civilization that way, if it hadn't been for the Gallacellans. They were core people. They lived on the worlds which we thought were bad. They didn't seem to like us much, and the feeling was fairly mutual.

The Gallacellans had been starfaring long before the human race had escaped its own system, and long before the Khor-monsa had begun to build their galactic society as well. Wherever we went, the Gallacellans had already been—at least to have a look. But they were a careful people. We found no trace of them, until we met them in the flesh. That was on Iniomi. Soon after, we met them on forty or fifty other worlds as well. Our civilizations overlapped slightly. But not much. What we called the heart of the galaxy, the Gallacellans figured almost as the rim. They came from the center. The humans and the Khor-monsa came from the outer reaches.

Iniomi got into all the history books as the world where we met the Gallacellans. Once there, of course, it got more than its due share of attention. Leucifer's inner worlds— II and III—attracted more people than they were worth on simple merit, and became thriving worlds despite the fact that life on both of them was tougher than it was most places we chose to settle. The Gallacellans retained only a small base on Iniomi, for no apparent reason. We opened a small base as well, for purposes of communication, but the Gallacellans weren't very interested in communicating. They wouldn't teach anyone their language, and only permitted a few low-caste members of their own society to learn a couple of ours. A few centuries' conversation seemed to have done little for either race. A number of Gallacellan names had passed into human languages, but even that was *via* the interpreters, who provided human-sounding equivalents of Gallacellan clickings. People could click in a fair imitation of Gallacellan speech, but they couldn't click intelligibly. Hence words like Mormyr and Iniomi were Gallacellan in origin, but sounded human because the interpreters had made them over into human sounds for us.

The average Gallacellan is about seven feet tall, but he looks taller because he has big ears which stick upward from his head. At least, rumor has it they are ears. After several hundred years, we still don't know for sure. He has a face which might be yellow or brown, sometimes striped or blotched, the texture of wax. He has eyes in the back of his head as well as the front, he also has a mouth in the back of his head, but somewhat modified so that it doesn't look very much like the front one. One is for eating (the front one), the other is for talking. A Gallacellan usually turns his back on you to talk to you, but if you are another Gallacellan you have your back turned as well, so it doesn't seem rude. Because Gallacellans don't look at one another when they talk they have no need of facial expressions, but they sometimes use gestures to attract the attention of the hind-eyes, which habitually look at the sky or the ground. People have hypothesized that the Gallacellans have so many eyes and use them thus because on their home-world they were prey to a large number of natural enemies. This remains conjecture. The Gallacellan body looks humanoid, but is capable of movements which the humanoid is not. The Gallacellan's limbs are of varying size and multi-jointed, and his body can coil like a spring over its full length. It is presumed that the Gallacellans are remarkable athletes. The females of the species are similar in all respects save that they tend to be somewhat plumper than the males and do not make use of the coiling facility, if they have it.

Little is known about the Gallacellan character. They appear proud and xenophobic, but in no way hostile. They are simply incurious and unforthcoming. Charlot, of course, wanted the Gallacellans to participate in his project for intergrating alien and human modes of thought (as the Khor-monsa were only too pleased to do), but they refused. No one could have been more surprised than Charlot when the Gallacellan named Stylaster offered cooperation in return for Charlot's assistance in a little matter of salvage.

Which explains why Charlot was mad keen on my being able to take the *Hooded Swan* all the way down to the surface of Mormyr. Needless to say, I was by no means as keen on the project as he. I have quite natural reservations about risking my life, especially for no good reason. I had wanted no part of the *Lost Star* farce, and I wanted no part of this one, which seemed to me to be too close to a carbon copy for comfort. As far as I was concerned, if the Gallacellans wanted to recover the ship which had gone down on Mormyr, then they could go fetch it themselves, and if they were unwilling to do so, then they shouldn't have been careless enough to lose it there in the first place.

Normally, I wouldn't balk at the idea of helping out aliens, becaue I quite like aliens, but the Gallacellans were not by any means a likable lot. Ecdyon was the only one I'd ever had occasion to exchange words with, and I hadn't much liked the words—though most of them, I know, had been Stylaster's and not Ecdyon's own. I've allowed people to talk me into doing some fairly hazardous things in my time, but not when they used such insulting patronization as Stylaster.

As I walked the streets of the Iniomi spaceport—the human sector—I was doing some pretty heavy thinking. I'd had it fairly easy for a long time with respect to the piloting angle, and a very respectable slice of the two years I owed Charlot had been swallowed up. It seemed a great pity to waste all that time by digging my heels in now. If I'd been going to tell him to take a running jump, then I should have done it right back at the very beginning. On the other hand, Titus Charlot simply was not a reasonable man. I'd helped him out time and time again, yet he showed not the least vestige of gratitude nor any intention of refraining from jeopardizing my future—and, for that matter, the future of the other people who worked for him. The poorer his health became, the more determined he was to wring all that he could out of such time as might remain to him.

I was considering quitting, and it was a difficult thing to consider.

The wind, of course, had every confidence in our ability to do whatever we were called upon to do. He thought we were a great team, and that we were only just beginning to integrate. I thought he had delusions of grandeur. He'd been on the rock where I picked him up a lot longer than I had. One couldn't blame him for being glad to get back in the swing of things, and he was certainly a useful guy to have around, but no matter how fully I was disposed to trust him, the fact remained that I was me and that I was the one who had to decide what to make of me. There's a protocol to be observed in relationships with alien mind-parasites.

It was a cold night, and I wasn't in any fit condition to walk for miles—and the town didn't stretch for miles, in any case—so I stopped off at a small coffee shop to sit and brood for a while. It was dimly lit and I deliberately chose a shadowed corner in which to sit, but I knew I couldn't hide. There were only a dozen places on Iniomi where I could possibly be, and if anyone wanted to seek me out they'd be sure to find me eventually. I knew *someone* would come looking—it was only a matter of waiting to see who.

The shop was deserted—there was no night-life on Iniomi. Bleak worlds breed bleak people. Iniomi had no life, and the air was unbreathable except in the domes. The base was supplied from Pallant—the third world. Nobody really knew why it was still here—they'd given up their attempts to make headway with the Gallacellans generations before. But these human bridgeheads tend to cling somehow. People who can't stand it leave, and whatever remains becomes the population of the world. Bleak people, but people nevertheless.

The coffee was good. Real. Pallant, though poor, was a productive world. Not big enough for the companies to take over, but good enough to supply its own needs with a lot to spare. Small traders—such as Lapthorn and I had been—ran in and out all the time. Worlds like Pallant were the only places where they could make a safe living now that the companies were steadily absorbing everything exploitable.

The waiting was good, too. The room was warm, and the girl who was serving didn't attempt to bother me except when I called. She sat, too, reading. Patiently whiling the night away. I riffled a pack of cards, not even bothering to lay out a game of patience.

I don't really know who I was expecting. I hoped it wouldn't be Charlot, and I didn't think that it would be.

But Johnny might have come, to tell me why he'd lost his touch with the plasm and blown the flux-field, and to tell me that it wouldn't happen again. Not that he could be held to blame—he was as good with the drive as anyone could expect him to be. He was a good engineer. Sometimes the flux-field blows, and that's all there is to it. No one has perfect touch. That's why it would be so foolhardy to go back again, even if Johnny *could* do it just a little bit better. Next time, it might be me who blew it. Nobody's fault. I mulled over the things I might say to Johnny.

On the other hand, it might be Eve who came. Eve often came around, just to see how I felt. Eve had an almost morbid curiosity about my well-being, or lack of it. I was the man who knew her brother, the man who nearly died with her brother, the man who might have died instead of her brother. She was Lapthorn's ghost, haunting me. But not in any malicious way. I didn't mind Eve. I wouldn't have minded if it had been Eve who came through the door, looking for me, wanting to talk to me about what was on and what might yet be happening.

As things turned out, however, it was Nick who came. Perhaps he'd been sent, perhaps they had all talked it over and decided it had better be Nick who tried to ease me back to a state fit for human company. Nick was my friend. Ever since the clash of loyalties had come out my way on the world in the Drift, Nick had reckoned himself my bosom buddy. But he knew I didn't see things the same way. He knew there was something between us—a ship. He always wanted to remove that obstruction to the true communion of our souls, because he was a guy who needed very much to like and be liked, but I had never permitted it. A matter of principle.

"You ought to be seeing the doctor," he said.

"I oughtn't to be in such bad shape I need a doctor," I said.

"This means a lot to Charlot—getting the Gallacellans to break down their wall of silence."

"It's not a wall of silence," I said. "It's a wall of indifference. They don't like us. They never have. Nobody can blame them. Their only interest in us is keeping us from interfering with them. They don't want to know about us and they don't want us to know about them. That's fine by virtually all the human race except Charlot. They're playing him for a sucker. They're using him, or attempting to. He knows it, and it makes him angry. He also knows he can't pass up the bait, and that makes him angrier. We'd all be better off out of this."

"You're going to try to use me against him," said Nick.

I nodded. I put the cards back in my pocket.

"Suppose I take his side?"

I drew a rigid finger across my Adam's apple.

"Could it be done?" he asked.

I hesitated. "Perhaps," I admitted after a while, figuring that earnest sincerity was the best line to take with a man like del Arco. "Perhaps it could. Getting down is the tough bit. Once down, it's easier to come back. It's always easier accelerating than slowing down. But there's no man in the galaxy up to it. Not Johnny, and not me. We're both good. But a man can only do so much. And I'm a spaceman, remember, not a deep sea diver. Atmospherics is not my specialty. Down there, my reputation doesn't count for much. I'm scared, Nick. For me and for the half-dozen others who die if I make a mistake. I'm not a young man, Nick—you know that. I can't take the responsibility of diving back into that Hell's Kitchen. I can't and I won't. If you decide that you *can* bear that kind of responsibility, you can give me orders. You're the captain. I won't obey them, and that will put me on the spot. Alternatively, you can tell Titus that it can't be done. He can sack you, but that's all. Ultimately, the authority is yours. That's the law."

"I don't want to lose the *Swan*," he said. It was an empty statement. The *Swan* wasn't his, for all that he carried master's papers. He wasn't even a spaceman. I think maybe he had always wanted to be one—all the time he was growing rich building ships—and I think the fact that he was nominally one now was genuinely important to him. But "genuine" is a relative term.

"Titus Charlot is a bad man to work for," I said.

"He's one of the most important men in the galaxy," he replied.

"So what," I said. "He isn't going to leave you his money, let alone his place in the history books. What difference does it make whether he's a big man with the Library or a tramp from the far rim? He's a bad man to work for."

"You did all right on Pharos."

"I'd have done just as well if I'd never seen Pharos. OK, for a while back there we were side by side. But I'm not fool enough to think that was forever. Titus is using us just as the Gallacellans are trying to use him."

"There'd be a queue a mile long to run the *Hooded Swan*," he observed.

"So let them have it," I said. "There's no point in being a sad dog in the manger."

"Would you do that?" he asked. "Just like that? If you weren't tied to Charlot by a millstone for two years, would you just cash in your chips and run, leaving the ship to the next man in line? And laugh all the way? You love that ship, Grainger, and I know you do."

Well, he was right, of course. But he was also wrong. Given the chance of an honest choice between attempting the Mormyr landing and giving up the ship, I'd leave the ship, I thought. But how could I be sure, without the honest choice? It was the pressure that made things so difficult.

"We might make Charlot see sense," I said. "If we tried together."

"You and me against the vast storehouse of Gallacellan knowledge?" he said.

He had a point.

"He's an old man," I said quietly. "He can afford to take chances with his own life."

"Just a minute ago," Nick pointed out, "you were crying about how you aren't so young yourself."

"And Johnny?"

"Johnny wants to try."

"Johnny's a reckless fool. What about Eve?"

Silence. What about Eve, indeed? I wondered whether Nick was in love with Eve, and decided that he probably was. No chance. No wonder his judgment was somewhat impaired.

"You know," he said, after a pause, "I can't bring myself to believe that *you* care all that much about Johnny and Eve."

I shrugged. "Maybe," I said. "I'm a selfish bastard at the best of times. If I were offered a chance to sacrifice my poor life for both of theirs I'd probably pass it up sooner than say thank you and die happy. I'm no hero. No hero at all. I'm looking out primarily for my skin. Fair enough. But what I say is true. Whether I care isn't so important . . . do *you* care?"

"I care," he said.

"That's what I thought."

I knew I had him. He was all mine. He wasn't going to be handing out any awkward orders. The Gallacellans could do their own dirty work and Charlot could have an apoplectic fit. Too bad.

We stared at each other for just a little longer. Then he looked down, and stirred his coffee slowly. The cup was half empty.

"Are you coming back to the doctor?" he asked.

"Maybe," I said.

"You want me to leave you alone?" he asked.

"What's the use? No sooner would you be back at the *Swan* than someone else would be out here to have a heart-to-heart."

"*They* care, you know," he said.

"I know," I told him.

"Reckless fools or not," he added, almost below his breath.

"I don't think I could stand a man-to-man talk with Johnny just now," I said. "It would be a mite too wearing. And as for . . ."

"All right," he said, "all right." He picked up the cup and drained it to the dregs. He stood up.

"Well," he said. "Are you coming back to see the doctor or aren't you?"

I guessed so. I stood up.

"He might invalid me out," I said, ruminatively. "What a tragedy. A great career nipped in the bud. Nothing so pathetic as a grounded starman."

But it was really a sour and bitter joke, and I didn't like it much.

We went back together, through the cold, shiny night.

We met a low-caste Gallacellan at the gateway to the shipyards, and I looked at him, wondering if it might be Ecdyon, and whether I ought to say hello if it might be. But he ignored us, so we followed the same policy.

The lights were still blazing inside the *Swan*, and Charlot was hovering in the corridor, obviously wanting to say something. I was tempted to pretend to be a Gallacellan and walk past him without the slightest tremor of recognition, but I couldn't make it. We paused to let him have his say.

"Stylaster said before he left that he hopes you make a complete recovery," Charlot told me.

"Well," I said, "that might be very nice of him. On the other hand, it might not. Did he happen to say *why* he expressed such a kindly interest in my well-being?"

"The doctor is waiting for you," Charlot said, without much trace of expression.

"Now there," I said, "we are on safer ground. I *know* why he shows a kindly interest. He wants his fee."

"You need sleep," said Charlot. Out of the corner of my eye I could see Captain delArco nodding puppetlike agreement. Well, so what? I did need sleep.

"We'll meet again in the morning," said Charlot. "We need a long talk about the near future."

"Local morning or real morning?" I asked him. We hadn't been on Iniomi long, and the time change had been an awkward one.

"I'll have you roused when we're ready," he said.

"Fine."

"One more thing."

"Yes?"

"Don't wander off like that again. The regulations state . . ."

This time I had no difficulty at all in forgetting he was there and going about my business. But even as I went back to my cabin, I knew that the affair wasn't settled yet by any means. Charlot was going to fight for this one. Tooth and claw.

3

I woke up in the morning without anyone having to come to rouse me. I was in no hurry to seek out my fellow crew members and hasten the painful postmortem on the events of the previous day. I made myself look human, and began the somewhat lengthier task of making myself feel human again, and I waited for the knock on my door. It seemed to be a long time coming, and when it did come, it was not who I expected.

It was, in fact, the Gallacellan Ecdyon. He introduced himself formally but I could tell by his clothes that he wasn't Stylaster, and so far as I was aware we had no other Gallacellans on board yet.

"Stylaster wishes me to ask whether you are fully recovered," he said, once I'd got over my surprise and he'd had time to turn his back.

"I'm not as bad as I might be," I told him.

"Stylaster wishes me to ask when you will be ready to make another attempt."

I narrowed my eyes. I knew this wasn't on the level. Stylaster might well have asked of Charlot whether I was fully recovered, and Charlot might well have referred the interpreter to me. But the idea of Stylaster addressing a question to me—whether he used an interpreter or not—was just not credible. Gallacellans are very much aware of status, and once they have a status situation sorted out they talk to the man at the top and him only. Real Gallacellans, that is—Ecdyon, by virtue of the fact that he had learned foreign languages in order to converse with aliens, was a demoted Gallacellan, almost an alien himself but Gallacellan enough to be a go-between.

"I'm not going to make another attempt," I said.

"Stylaster wishes . . ." he began.

"What do *you* want?" I asked him.

His big yellow hind-eyes blinked. One at a time. The small black pupils widened slightly, then contracted again. I got the idea that was phony too.

"Charlot sent you, didn't he?" I asked him.

"No."

"Stylaster didn't."

"Stylaster wishes me to know what is happening at all times."

I saw what he meant. "He gave you an open brief to ask whatever questions you might need to ask, and he left it up to you to decide who to ask, what, and when? That's interesting. What made you come to me?"

He paused for a moment, then said: "My observations have led me to believe that it is not always the human with the highest status who determines what is to be done."

I stared at him. "That's clever," I said. "That's really clever. Alien languages, alien ways of seeing. Stylaster *couldn't* bring himself to believe that, you know. He just couldn't." It suddenly dawned upon me why the Gallacellans allowed so few of their people to learn alien languages, and only the low-status people at that. A status society needs ultimate stability. Limitations even on ways of thinking. I remembered that rumor had it the Gallacellans evolved from a prey species, not a predator or a facultative predator. They were not individualists. I wondered whether I ought to offer Ecdyon a few hints on how to organize a revolution.

"What will happen if you will not guide the ship down to Mormyr?" asked the Gallacellan.

I sat down on the bunk and looked up at him. "Have a seat," I said. But Gallacellans don't sit down. He interpreted my invitation somewhat liberally and coiled himself up. To me, it looked painful, but he was built for it. The net result of the operation was that he ended up with his eyes at about the same level as mine and his body contorted beneath his loose robe. I could imagine him as a sort of gigantic snake. But his black robe was discreetly voluminous, decorated with blue and gold, and actually very handsome. He didn't look in any way repulsive.

I thought about answering his question. Then I thought that I might be passing up a chance to learn something interesting, and I decided to fence.

"I'll tell you what will happen if you'll tell me what will happen," I said. He blinked again. This time I was sure it was deliberate.

"Yes," he said, without hesitation. I wondered briefly whether he knew what I was after. Gallacellans were reputed to be remarkably shy of giving away information.

"OK," I said. "Here's how it is from our side. As you seem to know, we have only the one ship capable of doing what you want us to do—which, I presume, is to land on Mormyr and get you and Stylaster to this ship or whatever that's down there. Now, if I can't take that ship down there, effectively no one can. There are some men who might have the ability—men as good as me—but once they find out I refused to take the ship down they'll refuse also. To some extent it's a matter of etiquette, but primarily it's a matter of respecting my judgment. Ergo, if I don't go, nobody goes. Your ship—or whatever—stays there. The *Sister Swan* will be operational soon, but that won't make any difference. I don't want to boast and say that if I can't do it, nobody can—but I'm pretty sure that if I don't do it, nobody who can *will*."

He remained totally impassive, not bothering to blink. "It is a ship," he said, obviously willing to fulfill his part of the bargain. "Its name is the *Varsovien*. It was left on Mormyr nearly a thousand of your time-strips . . ."

"Years?"

"Years. A thousand of your years ago."

"It was left," I quoted. I didn't like to interrupt, but I wanted to get things straight if I was getting them at all. "It didn't crash?"

"No," he said. "It was abandoned."

"And now, after a thousand years, you want it back. Why?"

"I do not know."

I knew he was telling the truth. The underhanded bastard. But perhaps not. A little information was better than no bread, and I hadn't actually told him anything that was phenomenally useful. I paused for a moment, trying to frame another question in the most useful possible way, when the door opened. Ecdyon was sitting behind it and it dealt him a firm blow which knocked him over. Johnny literally bounded into the cabin.

"What the fucking hell do you . . .?" I began to shout, forgetting that one shouldn't swear in front of an alien, but Johnny wouldn't let me finish.

"Mayday," he said. "There's a mayday . . ."

"Where?"

"One-fifty mk out from the sun. About the same from here. We're closer than Pallant."

The fact that we were closer than Pallant didn't really figure. The *Swan* was far faster than anything that might be sitting around on Pallant Field. It was our pigeon.

"Drive-chamber, quick," I told him.

He disappeared back out the door, without even pausing to look at poor Ecdyon.

I helped the Gallacellan to his feet. He was making a peculiar noise with his back mouth, and seemed to be having trouble taking in air through his front one. I think he was winded.

"I am sorry," he wheezed, as he regained his full six foot ten. "Your air—it is rather bad."

"I dunno," I muttered, as I backed away, leaving him to look after himself while I pretended to be a lifeboat. *"We* like it."

I made the control room in seconds. I closed the locks,

and began to broadcast a warning to everybody within earshot via the klaxon. I checked to see that we had an empty yard, and found that there were people running for cover. I opened a circuit with the port authority.

"Tell me as soon as I'm clear," I snapped.

The officer was on the ball. He didn't bother asking questions.

"Hold hard," he said. "Information on the bleep."

There was a whine on the circuit as he transferred all the general information on the mayday call at high speed.

"Thanks," I said. Then, to Johnny: "Start countdown now, but be ready to hold her if we don't get the all clear."

"Eighty, seventy-nine, seventy-eight ..." he began, without preamble.

"How much burn can I use, port?" I asked.

"Regulation," said the officer. "Sorry, we just don't have the space."

"OK," I said. "Not to worry." Using a bigger thrust from the cannons to lift me would have earned a few extra seconds, but no more. As it was, we were better off blasting from Iniomi than the "official" rescue craft would be in lifting from Pallant, which had half as much again in the way of gravity drag.

While Johnny was still in the thirties, the port authority gave me the go-ahead to blast. By this time the whole ship was alive and alert. Ecdyon had staggered up to the control room to watch the action and Nick was at my shoulder. Eve was around somewhere, but neither Charlot nor the other Gallacellan had shown. I guessed that they were in conference somewhere on the ground, and that was why the crew pep talk hadn't materialized.

I took her up on a strictly regulation cannon burn, and I felt the flux come alive as we juggled the power.

"Right," I said to Johnny, "we're going to race the transfer and use every available second. Give me a hundred countdown and make sure that you have everything hot and set when we get to zero."

It wasn't really fair on him to cut his time like that—it

was pushing the limitations of the engine, and when you start pushing the limitations of the engine you're usually well beyond those of the engineer. If we missed the transfer we'd lose seconds instead of making them, and even though it would be my fault, Johnny was bound to think of it as his.

"Nick," I said, forgetting in the heat of the moment that we were on board and that he was the captain, "the info came in on a bleep. Pick it out and play it back to yourself. I haven't the time to take it myself. Just tell me what the situation is after we transfer, OK?"

He moved to comply. All the time I was speaking I was preparing to make the transfer. I was really pounding the flux, because I needed all the shields up. Leucifer was a matter-dense system and you can't go making tachyonic transfers in bad vacuum without a full complement of shields. As it was, we were bound to lose power when I went transcee. One shield at least was bound to crack, and unless Johnny and I were really on our toes we could bleed flux. After what the ship had gone through yesterday another bleed could wreck her—or at least ground her for a month.

But she behaved beautifully. The flux stayed perfectly balanced, my timing was dead on, and we were through the light barrier in no time. A slight movement of my ship limbs, the sensation of wind riffling feathers, and the shielding was back full, perfectly powered, dead even.

"Beautiful," I said. "Great work, son." Johnny said nothing. I kept concentrating and I kept accelerating. I searched inside the hood, but I couldn't see the stricken ship—or, at least, I couldn't sort her out from all the other junk that was floating around.

"Position?" I shouted.

Nick reeled off some figures, and I spotted her as soon as I had the region to look. I could see two other ships in the mid-part of the system. One was near Pallant and was presumably the boat coming out in answer to the mayday. The other was also headed toward the emergency, but she was a long way out, coming in from an outer world, or from outside the system.

I covered the distance between Iniomi and the injured ship in a matter of minutes. The junk that was all over the system didn't try to get in my way, and with the special faculties of the *Swan* I was virtually able to ignore the particles strewn along our path.

"Count me down to back-transfer," I told Johnny, and while he was coming down from a hundred Nick gave me the essence of what he'd learned from the bleep.

"It's a yacht called the *Saberwing*," he said, "privately owned on Pallant by a man named Ferrier. Crew of three. Mayday came in only a few minutes ago, but the mayday signal gave no information except the name of the ship. Either a bad captain or ... anyway, no way of knowing what's wrong."

"What a moron," I said. "What's he expect? Am I supposed to board him or what? We'll have to call him when we're subcee. Perhaps he's transmitted more while we've been on our way. I don't suppose he's expecting anyone for at least an hour. We must be taking minutes off the galactic rescue record."

The transfer down was as easy as the transfer up. Within five minutes after returning to subcee I could be knocking on the *Saberwing's* front door. It was a brilliant piece of flying, though I say it myself.

I opened a call circuit wide, so I could talk to the ship coming out from Pallant while she was still below transfer if I failed to reach *Saberwing*. At the same time, I asked Nick whether *Saberwing* was a p-shifter and whether we had any clue at all about what might be wrong.

"She's a p-shifter all right," he told me. "But there's no indication at all about the trouble."

"Can't be flux, anyway," I muttered. That was a relief. At least she wasn't going to blow up on me, and she wasn't going to be so hot as to be impossible to approach. P-shifters don't have many advantages—you can't take them hardly anywhere—but at least they go wrong discreetly.

I invited the *Saberwing* to communicate via the link, but there was no reply. I invited anyone to communicate, and got an answer from the ship that was coming out from Pallant.

"This is *Gray Goose*," was the message. "Bleeping data." Fast pause for a bleep, then: "We have no additional information. Transfer due in twenty seconds."

"Thanks," I said. "Go ahead. See you soon."

Nick automatically picked up the bleep and played it back.

"It's only her identification," he said. "She's the local police boat. Doubles as ambulance and lifeboat. Man in charge is Captain Corey. That's all."

It wasn't much.

I decelerated as I approached the *Saberwing*. She was drifting at a low velocity. I matched, and began to maneuver myself alongside. I sent out a couple more appeals to the ship, but there was absolute silence.

"What do I do?" I asked, of no one in particular. Having come so far so fast, I was tempted to don a spacesuit and rush over there at a sprint, but people have been known to get into trouble by acting headstrong like that.

I called up Pallant on the circuit. I told them who I was, and pointed out that it would be the best part of an hour before the official vessel could get here. I asked them for advice.

"Ferrier is a very important man," said the officer on duty at Pallant, without bothering to relay my message back to his own superiors. "I think we'd all be grateful if you could render what help is possible right now."

All in all, it wasn't very helpful advice.

"Captain," I said. "What do you reckon?"

"We'd better board her," he said. "I'll go, with Eve."

"Hold on there," I said. "If there's any boarding to be done, it had better be me that does it."

"We don't want to risk you," said delArco. "If we get into trouble too . . ."

"There's a rescue ship already on the way," I pointed out reasonably enough. "And if we leave Eve the *Swan* still has a complete crew. You can come with me if you like, but I've *got* to go. I'm the only one who might be capable of dealing with whatever's wrong over there."

"OK," he said, "You're in."

I took a last look around inside the hood before peeling it off. The *Gray Goose* was transcee and making good progress. The other ship was also making a beeline for us, and she was fairly close. But I couldn't see where she might be coming from. Certainly not one of the outer worlds. Did she just happen to be around? It was strange that she hadn't identified herself and neither the *Gray Goose* nor the Iniomi port officer had mentioned any other ship in the vicinity.

"What's wrong?" asked Eve, and I realized that I was hesitating and looking puzzled.

"Another ship," I said. "Coming for us like a bat out of hell. Could hardly be a passerby in a junk system like this."

"It's the *Cicindel*," said Ecdyon. He hadn't said a word since takeoff. Every eye was suddenly turned upon him.

"A Gallacellan ship?" I asked.

"Yes."

"What's a Gallacellan ship doing loitering in the outer system?" I asked.

"We have a base on Iniomi," he said, very reasonably. "Why should we not have ships in the system?"

"Why is he answering a mayday call?" I asked, although there was no real reason to be suspicious. Everybody answers a call for help, and if a Gallacellan spaceman knew no other word in an alien language, he would surely know what a mayday call was. On the other hand, though I knew what a Khormon cry for help sounded like, one Gallacellan click sounded just like any other to me.

"We're wasting time," said Nick.

"True," I said, shelving my suspicion and getting back to the matter in hand. "All right, let's suit up and go knock on the door. Eve, take the cradle. Don't get jumpy, but stay ready to move away fast if we tell you to. Johnny, make sure everything stays perfect. Don't lose concentration."

They both signaled their acquiescence with the slightly reproachful manner of people who do not need to be told how to handle themselves.

Nick and I descended to the lockers and suited up.

"Open circuit," I said. "May as well hear everything as it happens instead of waiting for the ship." On a suit set, of course, we could pick up calls coming in from Pallant or wherever, but we had only the power to send as far as the *Swan*—or the *Gray Goose,* when she down-transferred.

We went into the lock together, and locked our chains into the side irons. We had about a thousand yards of cable, but we were only a couple of hundred feet away from the *Saberwing*.

"You ever jumped before?" I asked him.

"Only practicing," he admitted.

"Well, it's exactly the same as practicing. Just don't get nervous."

"It's a long way down," he said.

"Ha ha," I said. I didn't think it was funny. But then, I'm a spaceman. He was basically a grounder.

We jumped together, but I didn't insult him by offering to hold his hand. Anyhow, if he had made a mistake, holding his hand would have only sent us both wrong.

We both made it. No trouble. We hit the skin and we both managed to stick. Nick cursed as he bumped—he'd pushed off a little harder than was necessary—but he covered up his imperfection. I began to worm my way over the skin of the ship toward the lock. It was a small ship—a pleasure boat or an interplanetary hopper. Maybe an executive craft—the Pallant officer had said Ferrier was a big cheese, and that usually meant big business, seeing as monarchies are out of fashion.

Inside of a couple of minutes I had the outer lock all ready to open, and I had my hand on the handle, when a message suddenly came in. It was aimed at the ship, but it was definitely meant for us.

"Pallant to *Hooded Swan*. Urgent message follows on bleep."

"Bloody idiot," I said. "Now we'll have to wait for them to play it back."

"Coming over now," said Eve, having rewound promptly.

There was a string of figures and identity codes that I didn't bother listening to. It was a police message directed to the port authority on Pallant.

"We have located Ferrier and the captain of the ship. The *Saberwing* has been stolen. Repeat, the *Saberwing* has been stolen. Advise caution."

"Well, well," I said noncommittally.

"What do we do?" said Nick.

"Thieves can get into trouble like anyone else," I said. "More likely to if they don't know enough about ships to handle them."

"Maybe we should wait for the police," he said.

"We're here now," I pointed out.

"We're not armed."

"We didn't come to fight a war. We came to help. If some poor idiot in there has buggered the engine he may be hurt. He's not likely to start laying about us with an iron bar—he's in no situation to be playing games like Custer's last stand. OK, the ship's been ripped off. So what?"

"All right," he said. "If you say so . . ."

He always was a remarkably passive captain.

I opened the lock. It was big enough only for one at a time.

"I'll go first," I said.

"No you won't," he told me. It wasn't that he wanted to be a hero, it was just that he didn't like clinging to the outside of a tin can 150 mk from the nearest *terra firma*. Who could blame him? I swung out of the way, and let him climb into the lock.

"You know how to operate it?" I queried.

"I'm not an idiot," he informed me. Sometimes, I wasn't sure. I sealed the lock behind him, and I felt the vibrations as he clamped it shut.

Then I waited. Time passed. The lock went through its full cycle, and I opened it again, and followed the captain through.

On the other side of the lock there was a square chamber, not the customary corridor. Nick was standing against the wall, with his hands held above his head in a ludicrous fashion.

A dwarf in a spacesuit was pointing a gun at him.

4

It might seem, in retrospect, that my actions of the entire morning were somewhat precipitate. From the moment that Johnny had kicked open my door I had been moving at top speed. Never once had I paused to think. This is not the way I normally conduct myself. It is true that I had things on my mind, and it is also true that events had piled themselves up with uncommon alacrity, but these truths did not prevent me from feeling an all-too-acute sensation of failure as I peered at the little man and his not-so-little gun.

We were both covered.

"This seems to happen a lot, these days," I commented.

"*You* can't complain," Nick said sourly. He was no doubt thinking that the last time he had boarded a ship the guy who had met him with a gun was me.

I turned my attention to the gunman. "Don't tell me," I said, realizing now what I ought to have thought of while I was still on the other side of the airlock. "You're on the run and you intend to hijack the *Hooded Swan* in order to make your getaway."

There was silence. I could see the little man's face—a particularly ugly face—moving inside the helmet, as if he were trying to speak to us.

"He hasn't got his caller switched on," I said to Nick.

"I don't think he knows how," he replied.

Well, I certainly wasn't going to step forward and touch helmets so we could speak. He'd probably shoot me en route. So I simply kept my hands in the air and leaned back against the bulkhead, with an expression of infinite patience on my face. The little man seemed to get even uglier. I glanced sideways at the pressure guage beside the airlock. It revealed that the air pressure was normal.

"Why are we wearing suits at all?" I asked Nick.

"How do I know?" he said. "You want to take yours off?"

"Ours not to reason why," I said.

There was a click as the gunman finally tongued the switch that opened the call circuit.

"Welcome to the conversation," I said, before he had a chance to speak.

"You're Grainger," he said.

That gave me pause.

"You were expecting us?" I asked.

"That's right. I've been waiting for you." His voice sounded thin and hoarse. "Now just do as you're told and everything will be fine." He picked up a bag from the floor behind him. "We're going back to your ship," he said.

"I don't suppose there's much point in my telling you that you can't possibly get away with this?" I said.

"No," he replied.

"I thought not. But there are one or two other formalities. Is there anyone else on board?"

"No."

"Is the ship really damaged?"

"No. But it will blow up in a few minutes."

"P-shifters don't explode."

"This one will," he told me. "I've put a bomb in it." His logic was devastating.

"We'd better go back to the *Hooded Swan*, then, hadn't we?" I said. I stepped toward the airlock.

"Not yet," said the little man. "I'm going first. If anyone on board your ship tries anything at all that I don't like, you and your friend here are still going to be aboard this ship when she blows. You understand me?"

"You listening, Eve?" I said.

"Yes," she said.

"Better do as the nice man says. Tell Johnny to put his gun away and stay in the drive-chamber."

"He hasn't moved," she said.

"That's good. After you, then, my good man."

I moved to the side. The little man walked past me into the airlock. As soon as the door closed behind him I switched myself out of the circuit and motioned to Nick to do the same. Then I touched helmets with him.

"With a reasonable amount of luck," I said, "we'll never see him again. Anyone who doesn't know how to switch on a suit caller doesn't know how to cross from one ship to another."

"Suppose he does make it?" Nick wanted to know.

"That's his problem. *Take this ship to Penaflor*, I suppose."

"And?"

"We take the ship to Penaflor. Or wherever. He isn't my problem. I don't care whether he gets away or not."

All of which seemed perfectly sensible. At the time.

After a decent interval, I switched my caller back on, and heard the hoarse voice telling us he'd made it and that we could come over, one at a time, and no funny business.

I looked at Nick, saw he'd heard, and shrugged philosophically. Nick crossed back to the *Swan*, and I followed him. The little man was waiting for us. He'd already taken off his suit. He was about four foot seven or eight, with a short neck and a big head. His face was lined, but he didn't seem to me to be very old—perhaps twenty-five, but no more. His hair was black and he hadn't shaved for a couple of days. His clothes were old and tattered, but not dirty. The bag he'd brought with him was bulging as if it held rigid things of odd shape and size. He watched us de-suit without a word.

"Control room," he said, as soon as we'd finished, motioning up the ship with his gun.

"Yes, sir, Captain sir," I said. I led the way, Nick followed, and the dwarf brought up the rear.

Once we were all sitting happily, he relaxed slightly, and looked around, first at Eve, then at Ecdyon. He seemed pleased to see Ecdyon, or at least amused.

"The *Saberwing* is timed to go off pretty soon," he said. "But before we go, there's something I want to do. Better let me get on with it as fast as I can, because if there's any difficulty we might still be here when she explodes. I have no idea what sort of damage will be done to this ship, but I imagine we won't get away scot-free. So, the less trouble I have, the sooner we can get out of harm's way. Now you—delArco, is that your name?—get out of the control room. You two, the woman and the alien, get back in that corner and stand still. Hold one another's hands and keep them visible. You stay put." The last remark, of course, was addressed to me, and indicated that I should stay in the cradle.

Nick left quietly. I knew he'd go straight down and get himself a gun, and give one to Johnny as well, and I couldn't see the point of letting him go. But the little man crossed to the door behind him, took two triangular wedges out of his bag, stuck them in the door above and below the handle, and gave them a couple of solid blows each with a hammer.

Simple, but neat. We wouldn't be interrupted by any heroes.

Then he came back across to the control console. He inspected it carefully, then moved around to the side of it, and opened one of the inspection hatches. He inspected the interior.

"Now," he said. "I'm going to have to put my gun down while I work. Don't get ideas. I'll know anything you decide to do before you do it. I know exactly what each of you is thinking. I can manage two minds at once. You just better stick to that Gallacellan's hands so he can't try anything. Just stay calm, and we'll be on our way soon."

"I wouldn't mess about in there if I were you," I told him.

"You let me worry about that."

"What are you going to do?" asked Eve.

He didn't answer. He put the gun down and began to pull stuff out of his bag like a magician pulling streamers out of a hat. He worked fast.

I answered Eve's question for her. "He's putting a bomb into the console," I said. "He doesn't think that the gun's enough. He wants to be able to send us all to hell with a flick of his finger. He's a real friendly character."

"What is his purpose?" asked Ecdyon.

"His purpose," I said, "is to evade the police boat that's heading for us at a rate of knots. He reckons the *Swan* can outrun her and outmaneuver her armaments. He may well be right, but I wouldn't care to guarantee the second part if the *Gray Goose* gets close. He knows my name and he knew Nick's. There was nothing wrong with the *Saber-wing*, he claims, so it's likely the mayday was a trap for us. I imagine that he wants very desperately to be out of this system in a hurry. Someone back home doesn't like him very much. I suspect he's been a bad boy. Whipping Mr. Ferrier's nice space-yacht is probably the least of his horrible crimes."

The little man picked up the gun again, and stood away from the hatch. He picked it up one-handed, dropped it into place, and closed the catch.

"My name's Maslax," he said. "And you're wrong. Ferrier's yacht was just to get out here. I haven't even started my career of crime yet." There was a very unpleasant edge to his voice.

"Fair enough," I said. "We are at your service. What do you fancy? Raiding the Caradoc treasure houses at Vargo's Star? Maybe robbing the Library at New Alexandria?"

Even as I said it, I could feel a very unpleasant suspicion creeping around in the back of my mind.

"Not likely," he said, and the unpleasant edge got worse. "We'll start with Leucifer V. Mormyr. I'm going after the *Varsovien*."

I felt suddenly rather cold. My eyes went toward Ecdyon. "You bastard," I said. "You bloody snake. This is your doing, isn't it? You cooked this up. You knew I wouldn't go down again. You knew you'd have to force me. Well, you can drop dead. I'm not going anywhere near Mormyr."

Maslax looked at his watch. "The *Saberwing* will go bang in less than three minutes," he said. "I suggest that you put some distance between the two ships, if you want to escape injury. I wouldn't want the *Hooded Swan* to be holed. I need her."

Wordlessly, I reached out for the controls. I took a quick look inside the hood and connected the electrodes to my neck. I gave her a quick burst which took us away from the *Saberwing* in a long arc. I put a few thousand miles of empty space between ourselves and the doomed ship, and then I let her slip back into a groove at low velocity. Then I ripped the hood off and turned my attention back to the Gallacellan.

"I know nothing about this," said Ecdyon, as soon as he knew that he had my attention. "Nothing at all."

I didn't know whether to believe him or not. If not Ecdyon, then perhaps it was Stylaster. But Stylaster would have had to use a go-between. Why not Ecdyon? Was this the sort of thing that Stylaster would even think of? The burst of insight began to look pretty faint in the light of reason. The Gallacellans were not, so far as was known, addicted to foul play. Quite the reverse. The idea of Stylaster using a man like Maslax for his own ends was patently ludicrous. And what did Ecdyon have to gain, if he were acting on his own behalf?

Maslax was looking on with obvious amusement.

"How did you know about the *Varsovien*?" I asked him.

"I can read minds," he said.

"Gallacellan minds?"

"No."

"Then how did you know? Only the Gallacellans knew about the ship."

"*You* knew."

"You're not trying to tell me you read it in my mind?" I said. "Is that how you knew my name? And Nick delArco's?"

"I know more than that," he said, with a hint of a sneer. "And about the *Varsovien,* I know more than you."

I looked back at Ecdyon. He was totally unreadable. Eve had let go of his hands once Maslax had picked up the gun again.

"Is that possible?" I asked the Gallacellan. "Could he know about the ship?"

"I have told him nothing," said Ecdyon. "I have never seen him before. If he knows anything, then he has another source of information—a Gallacellan source—or he really can read your mind, in which case he knows no more than you do."

"I know more," Maslax said confidently.

"Prove it," I said.

"I know about the Fenris device."

Well, he certainly hadn't got that from my mind. I'd never heard of any such thing. I looked at Ecdyon. "Well?" I said.

"I know nothing about any such device," he said.

Maslax looked disappointed. He might have been a very good actor, or he might well have thought that he was proving his point.

"Does the word mean anything to you?" I asked the Gallacellan.

"I know what 'device' means," he replied. "But I have never heard the other word. It is not a Gallacellan word. Its Gallacellan equivalent is quite meaningless."

"The *Varsovien* has a Fenris device," Maslax said definitely. "I *know* that's so. It's no good the alien lying. I know what I know."

"He isn't lying," I said. "He doesn't know what it

means any more than I do. I never heard the word either. It doesn't belong to any Earth language I know."

"Yes it does," said Eve.

I stared hard at her. Maslax looked at her too, dumbfounded.

"Well, don't just stand there," I said. "Tell *me.*"

"Fenris was a wolf," she said. "A giant wolf that ate up the moon. In the story of the twilight of the gods."

I had no difficulty in extracting the relevant phrase from what she said. *Ate up the moon* sounded very ominous to me. Very ominous indeed.

"The Fenris device is a weapon," I said.

"That's it," said Maslax, smiling. His teeth were bad. "I told you. I told you I knew."

He hadn't exactly shown us anything yet. But I was beginning to think that he might not be as crazy as he seemed.

The call circuit crackled. *"Gray Goose* to *Hooded Swan. Gray Goose* to *Hooded Swan."* The police boat was back subcee, and no doubt wondering what the hell was going on.

"Can I answer it?" I asked Maslax.

"Be my guest," he said.

"Hooded Swan," I said. "Grainger speaking."

"What happened? We saw the *Saberwing* blow."

"The *Saberwing* blew all right," I said. "There was this small matter of a bomb, see. And there's this small matter of a bomber. He's planted another egg in my control panel, and he's holding a gun on me right now. He has a little gimmick in his pocket which I suspect is the trigger for the bomb, but he hasn't felt disposed to threaten us yet."

"This is Pallant port," said a new voice. "Is the man's name Maslax?"

"Congratulations, Sherlock," I said. "The very fellow."

"Well, be careful," returned the man on the ground. "He's already killed two people. He's dangerous."

"Thanks a lot," I said. "I won't say you didn't warn me."

"Turn it off now," said Maslax.

"I think the policeman wants to talk to you," I said.

"Turn it off," said Maslax.

I turned it off.

"Now," said the little man. "Are you going to fly this ship to Mormyr?"

"In a word," I said, "no."

His face darkened, and the end of the gun barrel twitched. "You'd better be careful," he said. "If you take that attitude, people are going to get hurt."

"I've got this terrible suspicion," I said, deadly serious, although I maintained the tone of casual sarcasm which I've always found best for dealing with awkward situations, "that people could well get hurt anyway."

"Not you," he said. "Not any of the people on board. Not even the alien. All I want from you is a free ride."

"To Mormyr."

"To Mormyr," he confirmed.

"That's no free ride," I said. "It's not even cheap. But it does remind me. We were talking about Mormyr and the *Varsovien* when we were so rudely interrupted. Now you've invented this thing you call a Fenris device . . ."

"I didn't invent it!"

"Ecdyon," I said, "am I right in thinking that the Gallacellans do not use weapons?"

"Yes," he said.

"Am I right in saying that there is not a single Gallacellan ship in the entire galaxy which is armed in any way whatsoever?"

"Yes," he said.

"There is no such thing as a Fenris device?"

"I know of no such thing."

My eyes were fixed on Maslax. The dwarf's eyes kept flicking back and forth from Ecdyon to me and back again.

"It's a lie," he said. "I know that ship is armed. That ship is armed with the most powerful weapon . . ."

"Oh, God," I said. "Space opera. A misspent youth."

The gun barrel twitched again. I resolved to be more

diplomatic in what I said. I allowed a quick margin for thought. Did it matter what I said? Could he really read my mind? There was no proof . . . if he had intended to hijack the *Hooded Swan* before stealing the *Saberwing*, then of course he knew my name and the captain's name. I thought of trying to jump him, but decided it was no good. I couldn't afford to lose, and even if he wasn't a mind reader he might still kill me. Then I'd never know.

—He can't read minds, said the wind. He's crazy.

I thought you'd died in there, I said.

—I've been thinking, he said.

Go do some more. I'm busy.

Maslax took the gimmick in his pocket between his fingers, but he didn't draw it out.

"You were right," he said. "This *is* the trigger. . . ."

—I think you ought to know . . . began the wind.

"And if you don't do as you're told . . ." Maslax was saying.

—. . . that your knowledge of Gallacellans is . . .

". . . I'll blow this ship to wherever the *Saberwing* went."

—. . . limited. They *did* have weapons.

I was confused. First things first.

"OK," I said, "I'll head for Mormyr. While I'm headed there, I'll think it over. Just don't panic."

I put the hood back on, and I began to move the ship into an arc that would take us somewhere near Mormyr. I accelerated a bit, but I didn't want to transfer. So far as I was concerned, it could take weeks to get there. I was in no hurry.

What was that you said? I asked the wind.

—Gallacellans used to fight. They gave up, but it was a deliberate policy. They certainly had armed ships at one time.

How the hell do you know? I asked.

—How do you think? he replied. I was one once.

5

A not inconsiderable amount of water had flowed under the proverbial bridge since the wind had first invaded (infected?) my mind. At first, I had been implacably hostile to the idea of housing a second mind in a skull which I seemed to be filling adequately all by myself. Eventually I had become reconciled to the idea, had endeavored to set up an amicable working relationship, and had even gone so far as to make free use of the wind's talents when my own seemed inadequate to the situation in hand. By this time I trusted the wind, and I even liked the wind. He was discreet, and occupied himself peacefully for most of the time, and rarely intruded himself when he wasn't wanted. We had both approached the problem of two minds sharing one brain like mature individuals, and we had it under control.

But all this should not conceal the fact that I was still—to some extent—scared of the wind. I knew by now that he wasn't going to take over my body and consign my persona to outer darkness, but I was still anxious that my own individuality should not be threatened by a mingling of our minds. For this reason, I allowed the wind to make use of my motor nerves and my bodily capabilities to the full extent of his talents, but I had never allowed him to interfere with the workings of my mind. One has to have a certain amount of privacy.

I knew that the wind had access to all my memories and all my knowledge, so far as he cared to make use of it, and he had volunteered to give me access to all his. I had refused. I had refused even to evince any curiosity about the nature of his being, his past history, or his future plans. Perhaps this attitude was slightly unreasonable—the wind, at least, felt that the fear from which the attitude derived was unreasonable—but one has to consider that the wind was a creature whose whole existence was dependent on the sharing of another creature's mind. While between hosts he was completely dormant. He was therefore perfectly adapted to the degree of commingling which he wanted. I was not so adapted. My mind was designed for individual existence. Thus, the blending which—from his point of view—was the true essence of mentality, might well—from my point of view—be the destruction of my identity. It is all a matter of perspective. These are not matters in which one is inclined to take a cavalier attitude and needless risks. I valued my ignorance of the wind, because that ignorance was my guarantee of identity. Perhaps I was missing a great opportunity.

Well, perhaps.

There are certain situations, however, in which ignorance is an expensive luxury. I knew perfectly well that the wind had held up this little snippet of information about his having been a Gallacellan in times past for strategic reasons—he wanted me to appreciate to the full what a fool I was to hold myself aloof from his mental resources. I also knew that he would volunteer nothing more. I would have to ask him what he knew, and I would have to say "please" if I wanted to use any of it. I didn't hold it against him that he should play the game in this manner—simply because he was resident in my brain didn't mean that he had to put my interests before his own.

So you were a Gallacellan, I said.

—That's right.

When?

—I don't know. Their system of measuring time isn't easily translated into your terms. I had no way of measuring time myself while I was trapped on the world on the edge of the Drift. But I'd estimate that the last time I looked through a Gallacellan set of eyes was about ... say, twelve hundred years. Give or take ...

Never mind. I get the idea. You were a long time stranded.

—Longer than you.

Just a bit. The Gallacellan crashed there too, hey?

—He was passing by, just like you. The distortion pitched him down, just like you. It was a long wait, but I didn't really notice it. One doesn't, you know, when one is in one's gaseous phase.

No, I said, I don't suppose one does.

I was giving fast consideration to the matter of how far I should take the inquisition. My curiosity about the wind's past history had been awakened to the full by his dropping that one hint into this one situation—as he had known it would be. How much did I need to know? How much did I *want* to know?

OK, I said, I'm hooked. How long were you a Gallacellan?

—Not long.

Only one host?

—Yes. The Gallacellan picked me up on my home-world. The home-world of my species, that is. They picked quite a number of us up, I believe. But not enough of us to make a galactic civilization. That will have to wait. Given a million years, though ...

You live that long?

—I won't. I'll die out here alone, unless I can get back to my home-world to breed, in which case I'll die there. Not alone.

The significance of the last words did not escape me. The significance of the whole story, in fact, was not escaping me. If enough of these things (I counted the wind a person rather than a thing, but he was in a unique position of privilege—the rest still ranked "thing") ever got out of their home-world on any sort of scale, not a mind in the galaxy would remain inviolate. The implications were far too vast for me to take time out to consider right then. There were smaller, simpler things which I needed to understand.

So what do you know about Gallacellans? I asked.

—All of it?

Not all of it. Just sort out a few choice tidbits that you think I might be interested to know. Things which might help me understand all this garbage about Fenris devices and scuttled starship.

—Well, he said, I don't know that I can help much. I just don't know. If you'd let me give you free access, well, it might save a lot of tedious dialogue, but for once I agree with you. In this particular mess, you can't spare the time—how long do you think it will be, by the way, before this fool with the armory realizes we're not getting anywhere? Anyhow. Gallacellans. When I was one, they used weapons. Not only that, but they were inordinately fond of weapons. As you know—or perhaps only suspect—the Gallacellans and their ancestors had a rough time during the evolutionary process. They lived on a hard world. Selective pressure was high, and for once it was highest with the underdogs. They evolved their intelligence faster and better than the predators and the ubiquitous scavengers. They began civilized life as a fugitive, defensive-minded, very order-minded species. It didn't take long for them to crack all their problems and invent big guns for dealing with any and all natural enemies. They slaughtered the lot and were inordinately pleased with themselves. This is history, you understand, and ancient history so far as my host was concerned. I'm adding a little persepctive for you so you can understand better.

Yes, I know. Go on.

—Well, as I said, the Gallacellans, when they first started carving out a galactic culture, were great fans of weaponry. Defensive weaponry, of course. But you know the old, old story. Defensive weaponry tends to be even more effective when used offensively. You can't imagine the interstellar chaos that resulted from the Gallacellan space wars. I wasn't in them. This is still history. Maybe I can't imagine. But my host could.

—At the time I was a Gallacellan, they were making a lot of fast headway toward picking up the pieces. There was nobody around to watch them—they had their area of the galaxy to themselves, except for a couple of promising races who got steamrollered in the wars. The Khormonsa and the humans were yet to arrive on the interstellar scene so far as the Gallacellans were concerned.

Something has happened between then and now, I said, reflecting on the utterly non-warlike Gallacellan civilization.

—Yes, it has, and I'm pretty sure I can tell you what. Unlike humans, the Gallacellans have an inordinately ordered culture. They have a strong sense of community. The sense of disaster which prevailed after the wars was far more acute than anything a human is capable of feeling—so it seems to me. The Gallacellans decided to give it up. Now, I know that to a human the idea of giving up war and weaponry seems utterly ludicrous. But the Gallacellans were never quite as underhanded or as predisposed to cheating as humans. I'm not saying that to knock humanity—not in the least. It's the way humans are and I accept that. I'm not sneering. I'm just pointing out that because humans evolved from a scavenger species they have certain characteristics which the Gallacellans—who evolved from a herbivore species—have not. The Gallacellans had the sense of community and the social order to do what the humans cannot. They gave it all up. They became, once again, a peaceful species. I think they retain a strong sense of shame—and this I can only analogize to the way the Khor-monsa felt about Myastrid. As you know, the Gallacellans are proud. I think the Gallacellans still remember their history—although I'd be willing to bet they specifically exclude the go-between caste from that knowledge—but they want to keep it to themselves. If you like, from a human standpoint, the Gallacellans are a race with a guilt complex. But you know that the alien standpoint can never be reckoned from the human way of thinking.

I know, I said. I was beginning to understand. I was probably the only individual in the whole galaxy who was privileged to know about the skeletons in both the Khormon cupboard and the Gallacellan cupboard. Lucky me. Was there a skeleton in the human cupboard as well? Of course not. We don't hide *our* skeletons—we display them prominently to scare away the neighbors.

And the *Varsovien?* I asked.

—Your guess is as good as mine, he said. You know what I know. You suspect what I suspect.

I did indeed. The Gallacellans had abandoned their weaponry. But they'd been just that little bit careful. They'd left some of it where—if anyone wanted it *enough*—they might just be able to get it back again. They couldn't build more—not with the whole race carrying around a sense of shame. Not yet, anyhow. Not for another thousand years, maybe, when the memories had worn a bit thinner. But suppose there was one tiny section—one caste, say—which was just shameless enough to guard the secret of where a few of the warships had been left. Places where no one would ever find them, but places from which a really determined—almost suicidal—man might be able to bring them back. Just suppose.

All that remained was just two good questions. One: How did Maslax know that the *Varsovien* was armed? And two: *Why did the Gallacellans want their weapons back?*

The second question was a very worrying one indeed.

I was worrying about it quite fiercely when I felt something cold at the back of my neck, in between the two sets of electrodes which connected my nervous system to the nerve net of the *Swan*. It was the barrel of Maslax's gun. He was leaning over my shoulder, looking at the instrument board. I flipped up one corner of the hood and looked at him.

"When are we going to get to Mormyr?" he grated. He

had been getting impatient while I was otherwise occupied. I could see that he hadn't liked to interrupt me while I was busy, but I could also see that he was angry. I swiftly debated the possible answers I could give him, and decided that the truth would serve.

"At our present velocity, you mean?" I said innocently.

"That's right," he said.

"Oh," I said pensively, "I'd say . . . about a year and a half."

I was hoping that he was going to get hopping mad, and perhaps relax his guard enough for me to grab the gun and stop him getting to the trigger, which was back in his pocket.

But he didn't get mad. His face just drained of its color, and he looked to be feeling very cold. He took the trigger out of his pocket and he showed it to me.

"I've had enough of your sense of humor," he said. "If we don't reach Mormyr soon I'm going to blow this ship like I blew the last. I'll give you exactly half an hour."

I could have made Mormyr in half that time, but I saw no point in telling him so. I thought it was time to test his reserve a little.

"You weren't aboard the last ship when it blew," I said. "You can't blow the *Swan* without blowing yourself with it. Now you and I both know full well that you won't do that."

He chuckled. It was a horrible sound. I thought he was just trying to scare me.

"You don't understand, do you?" he said.

"Well," I said, "*I* can't read *your* mind, but . . ." Thoughts began to strike me then, and I paused. If this crazy man really could read minds, how was it that he didn't know that I was heading for Mormyr at a snail's pace? How come it had taken him so long to figure out which switch turned on his suit caller? He could no more read minds than I.

"You can't read minds," I said, half bemused, half accusing.

Unexpectedly, I got the reaction I'd been hoping for

before. But there was no chance of taking advantage of it. He leaped backward from the cradle as if he'd been stung. I watched his fingers whiten around the barrel of the gun, and for a couple of seconds I almost believed that I was shot. But neither beam nor bullet came out of the gun. He'd moved his finger from the firing stud at the last moment.

"I can read your mind," he said, his voice thinning out into a hiss. "I know exactly what's coming out of your mind."

"Tell me," I invited.

"Hate," he said, putting some hate of his own into the way he said it. "Hate and fear."

"Well," I said, keeping outwardly calm and as offhand as was possible. "I must admit that you're not exactly my favorite person at this particular moment in time, and I'm quite willing to concede that the way you're waving that gun around is a little worrying. I might describe my mental state as apprehensive. But I'm not radiating hate and fear, now am I? Be reasonable."

"Hate," he said, and his fingers whitened again as he squeezed the gun barrel, burning me to ash in his imagination—but only in his imagination. "Hate and fear." He was still hissing slightly. But his voice was trailing off into a whisper.

"You can't read minds," I told him flatly. "You can't read a single thing in my mind."

—Be careful, warned the wind. He's crazy. He thinks he *can!*

Maslax looked at me as if I were a poisonous snake. "I need you," he said. "I need you. To take me to Mormyr. You're the only man who can. But I don't need anybody else."

He stepped back, half turning to where Eve and Ecdyon waited in the corner. Eve was seated now. Ecdyon was still standing, slightly behind her. Maslax grabbed Eve by the wrist, but only with two fingers, because he had the bomb-trigger in the same hand. He yanked at her. She stayed seated, freeing her wrist without difficulty. Maslax spun, and jabbed the gun into her face.

"Get up!" he commanded.

Eve sullenly rose to her feet.

"We're going to Mormyr," said Maslax. "Fast. Otherwise I'm going to kill her."

I didn't know how far I dared push him. It was Eve's life at risk, and if he was as crazy as he seemed he might well kill her.

"You need her too," I said. *"I* need her, if I'm going to take this ship down on Mormyr. I can't do it without shots. She's the only one who knows which shots to give me when."

"You can tell the alien," said Maslax. "I mean what I say. Any more trouble and I'll burn her before your very eyes."

I shook my head. "Kill her and we'll never get down on Mormyr. There's just not time on a drop like that to give orders and explanations. It has to be done fast and smooth and exactly right. Without Eve, I'd never make it. I wouldn't stand a cat's chance. *If you can read my mind then you know that's true.*"

That caught him. It was a good line. I could see the doubt in his face, but I knew that he couldn't admit that doubt in his own mind. He had to make up his mind now. Was Eve expendable or wasn't she? Either way, I'd know. If he didn't believe me, he'd keep using her. Either way, she'd stay alive.

He sneered at me, and I knew the news wasn't good. He threw my gambit back at me. "I can read your mind," he said. "You can make it without the shots. You know you can make it. You think you're the best there is, It'll hurt you, but you can make it. We don't need the woman. So make up your mind now. Do we go to Mormyr, or do I kill her?"

"We go to Mormyr," I said.

I turned back to the controls, set the hood back in position, and told Johnny what to do on the way to transfer. Even while we were building up to the transfer I was considering what a hideous mess we were now in. By taking the line of argument I had I had put myself in a difficult position. By claiming that Eve was necessary to the drop, I had tacitly, without thinking, conceded that a drop was an actual possibility. If I'd thought faster, I'd have claimed that the drop was impossible, and invited him to blow the ship, as one way dead was the same as another. But would that have worked? Wouldn't he have begun to shoot one at a time? Would I rather try the drop than that? I thought fast, but no matter how fast, it looked as if I was going to have to brave the storms of Mormyr for a second time. And for what? For a crazy midget.

Once I'd made transfer, I had a few spare minutes. I thought I'd try to reason with him. I had no great hopes, but I had to try.

"Look," I said, "it's just not worth the risk. Even with Eve and all the shots just right, there's only one chance in ten I can get down to the surface. And if I can't hold her perfectly steady, she'll tumble, and we'll be stuck down there until we die. And that won't take long, in those conditions. I know that ship might be worth a lot. But can't you see that no matter how much it's worth, it can't be worth the risks we'll be taking in trying to reach it?"

I heard Maslax laugh, but I didn't dare leave the hood while we were transcee in order to look at him.

"It doesn't matter if your ship is down there for all time," he said. "We can all come back in the *Varsovien*. I'll even guarantee to let you go before I take the *Varsovien* back to Pallant. You'll live, all of you, if you'll just do as you're told."

"It's still not worth the risk," I insisted.

"Oh, it's worth it," he said. "It's worth it. You don't understand. I keep telling you that you don't understand but you won't believe me, just like you won't believe I can read your mind. They never believed me. Not any of them. They never took any notice. But I *knew*. I *knew*, because I could read their minds. They thought they could keep it from me. They thought they could block me out of their minds by just not looking at me, just not seeing me.

But they didn't understand. It's worth it to me, to get the Fenris device. It's worth all of life to me. It's worth more than the world, more than the universe. You don't understand, do you?"

"No," I said. "I don't."

"I know what you think," he said. "I can read your mind. You think I want to raise the *Varsovien* for someone else. You think the Gallacellans are paying me. You think Ferrier's paying me. Well, Ferrier's dead, and so is that girl of his. And I never talked to a filthy alien in my life. Nobody's paying me for the *Varsovien*. I want it for myself. You think I want it so I can escape, don't you? You think I want it so I can run away from the police, run away and sell it to some other world. Well, you're wrong. I don't want the Fenris to sell. I don't want it to escape. I want the Fenris device to *use*."

"Use on who?" I asked faintly. I already knew.

"On all of them," he said. "On all of them. The whole world. Pallant."

6

"Johnny," I said calmly—I had to be calm, in spite of everything—"we're going down. I don't think there's anything else we can do."

"Whatever you say," he said.

"You've got to stay steady. Is the captain with you?"

"Yes."

"Then tell him to get out. Tell him to go lie on his bunk and pray. I don't want him in a position where he might so much as catch your eye. OK?"

"All right, Grainger." Nick's voice floated up from the depths. "I'm on my way."

"Good. Now, I'll tell you what I'm going to do. Instead of going in on a long arc, like I did before, I'm going to go straight in. A vertical dive at high speed. I'm not going to pull out until I hit the garbage in the last few thousand feet, and then I'm going to pull out so that the storm wind sits on my tail, and I'm going to keep it there. That way I think I can cope with all the dirt and the vapor. If the wind changes while I'm pulling out, we're dead, but it'll only be a matter of seconds, and I think that chance might owe us that much. Now you'll know when I go into the curve because it will hurt me and I'll probably scream. If and when you hear me, you keep that plasma in the web—because if it bleeds it won't just leak, it'll explode, and there'll be one dead Johnny in the drive-chamber. The rest of us will survive you by about a second and a half. Now, you understand what I'm going to try to do?"

"I get it," he said.

"Fine. Eve?"

"I know. Just the stim. When you give me the word. It's going to hurt you, you know—hurt you badly."

"That's what I'm relying on," I told her. "Nothing like pain to sharpen up the reflexes."

"Or paralyze them," she said.

"That's another concession that chance owes me," I siad. "I won't seize up."

"Get on with it," said Maslax.

"You're sure in a hurry to die," I commented.

"Nobody's going to die," he said.

"How many people are there on Pallant? Twenty million? That's a lot of nobody."

"It's all nobody so far as you're concerned," he told me. "You'll live, and so will your friends."

"Count me down," I said to Johnny. I had already matched periods with the planet. I was directly above the spot that Stylaster had wanted me to aim for the day before. It was a real hell-hole down there.

Johnny was counting through the fifties.

"And you better all remember one thing more," I said. "I'm going down fast—I'll have to keep the shields up. But there's so much mass in the atmosphere I'm bound to lose one, maybe two, even in a matter of seconds. The rest will be stripped when I pull my daredevil trick at the bottom. Now, when the shields finally go the gravity will go with them for a second or two. There'll be a down all right, but it won't be the down you're used to. Make sure that you're all absolutely secure. Especially you, Maslax. I don't want you to hit that trigger by accident."

"We're all strapped in like good boys and girls," the little man assured me.

Johnny reached the twenties.

"We're on our marks," I said, and I gritted my teeth to keep from saying anything more.

I powered the cannons, building up thrust and loading the flux, and I flipped the ship. Down we went, plummeting like a stone, faster and faster.

It was only a matter of seconds, but seconds can be terribly long and terribly full. I had the wind to help me and he would do his utmost, but nerves are nerves, and the ship's nerve-net was designed to be sensitive—sensitive enough to alert me to mass densities many orders of magnitude smaller than those I would be crashing through. It was going to hurt me—and it was going to hurt the ship. Coming up might be a lot easier than going down, but in a crippled ship it could be just as fatal. But I intended to bring back the *Swan,* no matter what Maslax's plans might be.

Johnny reached zero and we plunged. The drive screamed, but the flux was in perfect synch. I had the web down low to cover the deration. Our effective mass was tremendous, but that only meant we were falling faster. I didn't care about mass because I didn't intend maneuvering except once. I was betting my whole stack on one turn.

It was like diving into an acid bath. An acid bath with an undertow. I began to burn, and without the passage of any subjective time at all I was consumed by flames. At the same time I felt the hands of the atmosphere smash into the shielding, millions of them, chopping it away, shattering the force-lines into flinders. All of it hit me at once. It was like dying.

There was only one instant in that dive. I don't know how many times the clock ticked, how many times my heart beat, because from the moment we hit the air I was no longer in the same world as the clock and the heart. I was suspended in eternity, blasted right out of body and mind by the sheer power that poured into the ship and which the reaction poured back into me. I was flying with the *Swan's* body, feeling with the *Swan's* senses, and I knew that if the *Swan* had had any mind, any identity except for me she'd have destroyed me for putting her through that dive. But I was she, and she couldn't destroy me because I wouldn't let her destroy herself. I held her still, plasma, discharge, and mind, and the wind held the stillness, and down we went, apparently forever.

Something inside me was still tuned to the instruments, but I have no idea what it was or how. Somewhere, there was a trigger to pull me out of the dive, but the trigger had to pull itself because all the "I" that I knew about was totally bound up with that wave of agony and that shearing shield.

We lost one, vanished just like that, gone. There was no bleeding of either power or balance. There was just no time. We were suspended in time and balance. The second shield followed the first and I clamped the deration syndrome and I froze the flux absolutely still, but not jammed, caught still in a stream of motion. There was a fugitive instant, which we almost reached, but couldn't quite, in which I'd have hit the light barrier without transfer and we'd have blown a hole in Mormyr that would have become one of the seven wonders of the universe, and the atoms that had been me would have been strewn from now until the very beginning of time.

Instead, the needle shot so much life into my arm that for just one tiny fraction of that timeless instant where I was suspended my heart and my brain were able to transcend those fires of hell and I blasted everything out of the cannons and cartwheeled the ship.

The shields just vanished, and they took up and down and all around with them, and for a moment we were *all* nowhere and nowhen. But I was already feeling for the wings of the storm and matching them to my wings and trying to find some kind of perfect harmony.

That was when chance, and chance alone, held the cards. If there had been no such harmony, if the storm into which I'd plunged had been real, absolute chaos, we'd have become part of the storm. Chaos. But the storm-wind was blowing, blowing everything before it, and we joined it, and all of a sudden there we were, deeper than it was possible to be in the atmosphere of Mormyr, making a few lousy hundreds of kph, in one piece, flux balanced and staying balanced despite the best efforts of the storm, slowing down, safe and well.

I was lost, lost in a maze of color, with all the devils in hell screaming in my ears, with steamhammers crushing me to pulp. But most of all the colors, blinding colors. I thought I *was* blind, or would be, but I realized what was happening. The overload had scrambled the whole sensory net. The ship and I were suffering extreme synesthesia. So was the wind. But my body was already programmed, and it was doing what was necessary. I was away no more than a few seconds, and when I got back I was still doing what was necessary.

I was feeling no pain. The threshold had been passed. The receptors in my brain had just cut out. Perhaps the wind had had to cut them out. For the next few hours, I would feel nothing as my body went through its programmed motions. Nothing at all. The sense of touch was simply gone. It would return, in time, and *then* I would feel pain—all the pain in the world, for hours. But by then I would be under an anesthetic. Knocked out.

It might take years off my life, but I wouldn't know very much about it.

Seconds later, we landed the ship.

We were down.

7

Thirty hours went by before the wind allowed me to come out of the coma. By that time, I was whole again. I felt terrible, but human.

I *said* it was impossible, I told him.

—It always feels worse than it is, he assured me.

It couldn't have felt worse, I assured him.

—Precisely, he said, It could have *been* a lot worse.

We couldn't ever do it again, I said. It'd kill me.

—We could do it twice weekly and earn a living, he told me. Practice is all. Without me, you'd have found it difficult the first ten or a dozen times, but after that—if you survived—you'd be able to handle it with equanimity.

He was a cheerful little bastard, sometimes. He was right—it does always feel worse than it is. But there are some feelings a man shouldn't have to undergo.

Never again, I said. Under no circumstances whatsoever.

—It's not over yet, he said ominously. The best is yet to come. Our kindly host is getting more and more impatient while we lie here recovering. Our friends are suffering all kinds of misery. There are agonies you haven't even contemplated yet.

I don't want to contemplate them. I just want to lie here and be ill.

—You can't afford the luxury. You need your mind for higher things. We have got ourselves into this mess. We have to think of a way out.

No way, I said. No way. I think I'll just die. Let Maslax blow the ship. We should have told him to go to hell up on top, and then at least I could have died swiftly and peaceably.

—If that's the way you feel, he said, you'd better go back to sleep. I'll wake you again when you're better disposed to consider the problem.

He did. In fact, he woke me three times more that day, but I was just too sick to think. I asked him to amputate my memories of the dive, I asked him to mask the colossal hangover I had. But he couldn't do either. The last time I awoke temporarily, Eve spoon-fed me a little. Prior to that I'd been on intravenous supply."

When I awoke for the fourth time, it was like waking from a normal sleep. When I was fully awake, I felt a sense of astonishment that I could be whole and well again. But the wind wasn't about to allow me to simply lie there and enjoy myself.

—You know what's going to happen now, don't you? he said.

No.

—Well, you'd better think. If you had spent more time thinking these last few days and less time rushing about and sleeping, we might not be in this mess.

OK, I said, tell me what I ought to know.

—Maslax wants to raise the *Varsovien*.

That's right. He has no chance. He doesn't know the first thing about spaceflight.

—So who's he going to take with him to fly the ship?

But I don't know how!

—He isn't going to believe that. In any case, that's not the point at issue. He's going to go to the *Varsovien* in the iron maiden, and he's going to take you with him. Once he's out of the *Swan*, we're going to have to jump him. We have no choice at all. Now, all I want is for you to think about that. Be ready for that. Pick your moment. I'll be ready. Just make sure you are. OK?

I promised him I'd keep it in mind. I got up and began to dress. Before I'd finished, Eve came in. Maslax was behind her, holding the gun. He smiled when he saw me—a great big beaming smile. One might have thought I was his only friend in the whole world.

"I'm glad that you're well," he said. "Very glad indeed. I've been waiting a long time. I think we're ready to make another little journey, now."

He was not ungenerous, mind. After some persuasion, he agreed to let me eat before we set out bravely to face the perils of the unknown. He also agreed that someone else could drive the buggy. We suffered a serious breakdown in diplomatic relations only when it came to deciding exactly who should go. Had we settled it democratically, there is no doubt the makeup of the expedition would have been considerably different. As it was, however, Maslax had the only vote worth mentioning, and he called the tune.

Thus, when the iron maiden rolled out of her harbor in the underbelly of the *Swan* she carried a crew of four. Eve was driving, and Ecdyon was in the front seat alongside her. I was in the back with him, the gun, and the trigger mechanism for the bomb. I knew, and he knew, that neither Nick nor Johnny knew enough about bombs to risk tampering with the one on the ship, but I wasn't so sure they wouldn't try. I hadn't told them not to, and secretly I was cherishing a fond hope that they might get reckless and lucky all at once and defuse the thing. At the same time, however, I could hardly avoid the corollary fear that they might get reckless without getting lucky.

We were all suited up inside the maiden—we had no illusions about the amount of risk we could safely take. The vehicle was built to take just about any amount of battering, but nobody had ever thought that she might have to run around on a world like Mormyr.

When I got my first look at the vaporous caldron into which I'd dropped the *Hooded Swan* I felt a sudden renewal of all the agonies of the drop. The synesthetic psychedelia that I'd experienced were represented here in living color.

The sky seemed to be about twenty feet above our heads, a boiling curtain of vapors that writhed from blue to gray to red. All the colors were very dark—though it was daylight here there was less light to see by than the stars provided at night on Iniomi—and they gave the impression of being spectral patterns in an oil slick. I had never seen a sky which gave the impression of being so *heavy*. It was not merely oppressive, it was positively claustrophobic. It was as though the ground was one surface and the clouds another, with the merest crack between them. And it was all too easy to conjure up the illusion that the crack was slowly closing, the sky slowly falling. I felt like a grain of wheat trapped between slowly turning millwheels.

And the sky was angry. There was no doubt about that. From point-blank range it spat raindrops and hailstones at us. The hailstones were often as big as chestnuts, and they shattered as they hit the maiden's steel carcass. They came from all directions, blown about by the wind which eddied madly this close to the ground and their bombardment sounded like fingers racing on drumskins. It was worse when the big ones hit the shield or the windows, because they they didn't shatter, but bounced instead, and made a dull thumping sound like a big bass drum booming steadily away behind the rattle of the kettledrums.

Needless to say, visibility along the ground was not too good. We had a fairly sizable patch of clearshield, thanks to the overlip that kept most of the rain off and virtually all of the hailstones out, but the vapors were thick enough to cut clear sight down to a matter of ten meters, and the gross irregularity of the terrain often cut that still more.

With a perpetual storm raging over it, and rain washing it, hailstones hammering it, I would have expected the terrain to be smoothed flat as a pancake, eroded into a perfect plain. But this was by no means the case. For one

thing the rock wasn't homogeneous, and it eroded at varying rates, so that all around us were squat, stubby projections twisted into the weirdest shapes, often holed or hon-
eycombed, like impressionistic statuary. The curves and
the swirling vapors could hardly refrain from suggesting
movement, but the movements all seemed to be impossible
writhings and wormings as though the statues were not individual shapes at all but were heaped multitudes of tiny
creatures—snakes and frogs and black fish.

In addition to the uneven erosion, the misshapen con-
figuration of the terrain was the result of continual volcanic activity and earth tremors. The crust of Mormyr
was very deep, but in its upper regions it was uneven and
unstable. Most of the tremors were inconsequential, origi-
nating far below us and at great distances, so that all we
perceived inside the maiden were slight shivers. No great
cracks appeared around us, nothing was broken. Only the
dust was really disturbed by the quaking of the earth—it
was shaken and stirred. It danced, in a region mere inches
above the smoothed skin of the rock, blurring the ground.

We had very little to fear from the volcanic erup-
tions—those we were aware of seemed very tame. No
mountains rose to hurl flames and magma high into the
air, though no doubt such mountains were not very far
away. All we saw were small slits in gullies slowly oozing
viscous liquid which turned the colored rain into colored
steam and which cooled and bubbled and cracked and
oozed in a constant but sluggish turmoil.

What I did fear more than almost anything else was the
lightning. Although we were not a tall target—the iron
maiden was not built to be proud, but to be discreet—the
projections that surrounded us were even less so. We were
able to choose low ground, for the most part, but we
dared not risk the gullies for fear of the magma that sim-
mered there. We had to compromise and do the best we
could. The lightning made patterns in the sky all around
us—when there were sudden sequences of burst, we were
caged by the light. The electric glare was the only thing
which penetrated the gloom of the ground-hugging

clouds—it was all that came to us from without our
stormy cocoon.

Needless to say, driving was extremely difficult, hazardous and slow. Eve was a good driver, but had never
driven in conditions which were remotely similar to these.
Ecdyon navigated for her—we knew exactly where the
Varsovien lay—but we made painfully slow progress.
Even Maslax, however, had to curb his impatience under
the prevailing conditions. We had less than forty miles to
go, but it was going to take us several hours and there was
no way of getting around the fact.

We maintained a dogged silence for the first hour or so,
but the silence became almost as oppressive as the sky. It
was broken only by Eve's occasional muffled curses as we
lurched or had to back up to find another way through a
particularly bad patch. Occasionally Ecdyon would murmur something—an instruction, a comment—but he
mostly just pointed with his hands, owing to the fact that
he was in an awkward position. Gallacellans, as I've said,
were not built for sitting. In order to fit in his seat he had
to bend, and while he was folded he couldn't coil. This
meant that his head was stuck in a single orientation, and
couldn't swivel as the occasion demanded. His fore-eyes
were stuck in forward orientation, and his hind-eyes were
pointing backward, staring Maslax full in the face. This
meant that Ecdyon could conveniently address himself to
Maslax or me, but not to Eve. I knew that he must be terribly uncomfortable, but Maslax either didn't know or
didn't care; every time Ecdyon writhed himself into a
slightly different posture the little man moved the gun
around to threaten him.

At this point, I was pretty sure I could take the gun
away from him—with the help of the wind. But there was
one thing I hadn't considered. Maslax had deliberately
chosen a suit that was too large for him—one of the
Swan's suits instead of the one he'd had aboard the *Saberwing*. He'd adjusted the legs so he was able to walk com-
fortably, but he'd not troubled to adjust the left arm. This
meant that his right suit-arm was some five inches shorter,

and therefore he had five inches of empty space beyond his left fingertips. In this space, he was carrying the trigger-device for the bomb aboard the *Swan*. Thus, though I could take the gun off him if I was fast enough, there was absolutely no way I could stop him triggering the bomb and blowing up Nick, Johnny, and the ship. This made the situation very difficult. I only hoped that the fact that he was now effectively one-handed might cause him to fall and break his neck at some indeterminate time in the future.

Eventually, there came a time when I couldn't stand the silence any longer. In any case, I decided, it was time I went to work on Maslax again. They say you can generally talk lunatics out of crazy situations, and this was no time to be passing up an opportunity no matter how little faith I had in the old wives who were credited with the rumor.

"You know," I said to him, as though we'd just met on a bus, "I seem to be going through one of those periods when absolutely nothing goes right. All snap decisions and every one turns out to have been second best or even worse. Know what I mean?"

He looked at me somewhat somberly, but I think he was glad of the chance to direct his morbid attention away from the morbid landscape.

"You don't have to make any decisions at all," he said. "Just do as you're told."

"Ah," I said. "That's just it. What are you going to tell me to do? I've been sitting here examining nasty suspicions, you see, and it occurred to me that you can save me a lot of needless worry. You're not an idiot, now are you? You're not going to ask me to fly an alien starship?"

"I might," he said.

"You know I can't do it, don't you?" I said. "You can read my mind, remember? You know I don't know anything about alien ships."

"*He* does," said Maslax, indicating Ecdyon.

"Do you?" I asked the Gallacellan.

He didn't answer immediately, and it dawned on me

suddenly that he probably did. He'd not been attached to our little mission without a proper briefing. He probably did have instructions about how to lift the *Varsovien*. I wondered how likely he was to lie.

"No," he said. "I know nothing about the *Varsovien*. Stylaster knows. No one else, so far as I am aware."

Maslax didn't believe him any more than I did. "A ship is a ship," he said. "Even I can fly a spaceship. Even little Maslax. One of you can fly it. I don't care which. One of you is going to."

How about you, I asked the wind. You're the ex-Galla-cellan. Do you know how to fly it?

—You know me, said the wind. I'll try anything.

I did know him, as it happened. He was a trier all right. He'd not failed me yet. But . . .

"Tell me," I said, redirecting my attention to Maslax. "What gives you the idea you can read minds?"

His head was at the wrong height inside his helmet—his nose was where his lips ought to have been—but I could still see most of his face through the visor, and I saw something flow into his face the moment I mentioned mind reading. Perhaps it wasn't a good thing to talk about after all.

"I know what's in *your* mind," he said. "Your mind's full of it, like all the rest."

"All the rest of what?"

"Don't play stupid," he said, his voice grating harshly. "All of them. All the people."

"And what are they full of, Maslax?" I asked him, still pushing, to see what might happen. "Still hate and fear? Is it only hate and fear you can read?"

"Hate and fear's all there *is* to read," he spat at me. "It's all there is."

I shook my head, not dropping my eyes for an instant. "You know that's not true," I said. "You can't believe that."

"You don't know," he said fiercely. "You're not Maslax. You're not a cripple. You don't know what it's like when everyone who passes you on the street looks at

you as if you were an insect. You don't know what it's like when anyone who has to stand near you *recoils*. You don't know what it is to have everyone who knows you *despise* you. You just can't know. You don't know what other people's minds are like. You don't know what your mind's like. You tell yourself lies, just like there are lies coming out of your mouth all the time. You don't know. I do. I know what goes on people's heads. Hate and fear—yes, that's what I read. That's what's there to be read. Hate Maslax. Loathe Maslax. Maslax the crippled, crawling thing. That's what's there. You can't deny it. You feel it. Look at your own eyes. You hate me, Grainger, you and that four-eyed bug and that lady in the front seat who's trying so hard not to listen. You hate me, and you're afraid of me. Well, this time you've reason to be afraid. But I need you—*some* of you—and I'll let you go. Not the others. Not the ones who've got a lifetime of hate and loathing to pay out. Not them."

"Has it ever occurred to you," I said, quietly but gathering intensity, "that you might be *mad?*"

"Has it ever occurred to you," he replied, "that I might *not?*"

I had to admit that it hadn't.

"You're intending to kill—how many was it? twenty million?—twenty million people, and you want us to believe that you're sane?"

"The population of Pallant," he said, "is twenty-five million. And yes, I do want you to believe that I'm sane. I want you to believe that I have a perfectly respectable motive."

I looked at Ecdyon. Not a muscle was stirring. I still didn't believe that Ecdyon had nothing at all to do with this. Only a Gallacellan could have known about the warship—if there really *was* a warship, and only a low-caste Gallacellan could have put it into English. If the knowledge hadn't been given to Maslax directly—and I was prepared to believe *that*, at least—then it had come to him indirectly. Via Ferrier? Perhaps. But someone had rendered it into English somewhere along the line, and

Ecdyon looked like the prime suspect to me, despite his insistence that he knew virtually nothing about the *Varsovien*.

"You killed a man named Ferrier," I said to Maslax. "Did you have a motive for that, too, or did you just want to steal his yacht?"

Maslax coughed out a laugh. "Motive?" he said. "For Ferrier? I had all the motives in the world. I had years full of motives. I have a lifetime of reasons to kill Ferrier. I should have killed him years ago. I knew that I'd have to, eventually. I always knew."

"But if you'd killed him years ago," I said, prompting him, "you wouldn't have found out about the Fenris device, now would you?"

He was silent. Perhaps he was thinking over what I'd said. Perhaps what I said didn't make sense.

"It was only recently that Ferrier found out," I said. "What did you do, read it in his mind?"

"Yes," he said quickly, rising to the bait like a suicidal mackerel. "I read it in his mind. That's . . . when I knew, you see, when I knew that I could . . . had to . . . kill him. That was why . . ."

"You mentioned a woman," said Eve, keeping her eyes on the precarious way ahead. "What did you kill *her* for?"

I would much rather have continued trying to find out about Ferrier, but I didn't have a monopoly on Maslax, and in any case, finding out the right questions to ask was pretty much a matter of trial and error. Eve's question might yet lead to further discoveries.

Maslax was again reluctant to answer without leading, but I didn't know how or where to lead, this time. We waited.

"She was worse," said Maslax, finally. "She was worse."

"Worse than what?" I asked.

"Worse than all the rest. She was the worst. You just can't know what it felt like. You just can't know what pain a mind can feel . . . a wave of hate, pure *repulsion*. You just can't know . . ."

"Tell me what happened," I suggested, trying to sound

gentle—maybe even sympathetic. Either I couldn't manage it or it was the wrong ploy in any case.

"Shut up," he said. "Just shut up. Where's that ship?
We should be there by now. If you're trying to . . ."

The gun wavered, focused on the back of Eve's neck.

—Get him, urged the wind. But even he didn't sound
too confident, and we both knew that while the bomb was
inside his suit there'd be no getting to be done.

"She isn't trying to do anything," I told him. "Look
outside. This isn't a highway. We're a long way from the
ship yet."

He looked outside, seeming to notice for the first time
the colored storm that hid the world from us and battered
futilely at the body of the maiden. He looked down at the
ground beside the vehicle, craning his neck to sit up in
his suit and look over the edge of the window. He
watched for more than a minute, apparently fascinated by
the bursting of the oily raindrops and the swirling colored
dust with which they mingled, and the vapors that rose
from the dust and left it still dry.

"It doesn't ever stop," I told him. "It's a constant cy-
cling. Some of these rocks are very hot indeed. The atmosphere's very deep and thick, and the upper strata are
very cold. It's not just water. There's life up there, you
see. A kind of aerial plankton. We can't see it, not down
here. The individuals are so small—like dust motes
blown about on the winds forever. There are other life-
forms down here, but we won't see those either, in all
probability. They'll be in the cold-spots and the lakes—
not necessarily water lakes; that depends on the cyclother-
mic properties of the bedrock. This is high ground we're
on now. Over half this planet's surface is liquid of one sort
or another. Mostly sulfurous or hydrocarbon. A high per-
centage of the life-forms here will metabolize sulfur com-
pounds as well as—or instead of—carbon."

He looked at me soberly. I'd reeled off the information
as much to show off as anything else, but I had some
hopes of it putting him in a better mood.

"It's a hell of a place to spend your day off," I remarked, as he kept up his stare.

Lightning flashed almost overhead, and there was a peal of thunder like a broadside of cannon. We all jumped, and it broke the little man's stare.

"We could all die here you know," I told him. "Just because you have a gun and a bagful of bombs doesn't make you the lord of all creation, does it? Just because you have a gun and a cause—you can't wave that gun at the universe and say 'I want that ship lifted, give me a miracle.' We've already done the incredible once in getting down here. It's asking too much for us to lift the *Varsovien* as well. Even if we reach it."

But he wasn't going to buy it. He wanted that miracle, and if the universe wasn't going to provide it, via me, he was going to shoot us all, blow the *Swan*, and keep screaming at the storm until the moment he died. It wouldn't take long.

As I sat there looking at him I was suddenly consumed by a feeling that had hardly touched me even in all the most difficult situations of the last few months. I was suddenly consumed by the feeling that there was no way out, that whatever happened we were all going to die. Perhaps there was a moment in the Drift when I thought the same, perhaps when Michael faltered in his playing while we were keeping the spiders at bay on Chao Phrya. But at those times I was doing something, I still had cards in my hand to play. But was there any amount of card playing going to get us out of this?

No. Nothing short of a miracle.

It was at that moment, drenched with fear and despair and the futility of it all, that I decided I was finished. Paradoxically, I suppose, the moment when I thought that there was no hope was the moment that my decision about what to do finally fell into place. I had had enough of Charlot, enough of trouble. There wasn't a problem in the universe that Charlot didn't want in on. He didn't just want a hand in Destiny, he wanted to *be* Destiny. Well, OK. But I never wanted to be Destiny's right-hand man.

I never was a hero. I never was one to accept the troubles of all mankind. Let him hire Flash Gordon. I was finished. If the course of events was kind enough to throw me out of this thing alive, I resolved—firmly and finally, then I would quit, and Charlot could call down the vengeance of heaven, if he wanted to.

"We're going downhill," said Eve. "It looks better up ahead."

I returned my attention to the outside world. It did, indeed, look much better. The knobs of rock that had plagued us for miles were getting sparser and smaller. We were heading down at an angle of five degrees or so; the slope was getting smoother and cleaner. The wind howled just the same, and the thunder still barked, but it all seemed just a little more distant now that the way was clear for us. Even the visibility was a fraction better. Eve accelerated.

"How far away are we?" I asked Ecdyon.

"According to my calculations," he said, "we are within two hundred meters."

"How big is it?" I asked.

"I do not know," he said.

It was a futile question anyway, because by the time he'd answered, we could see it. Only slight glimpses, at first, and we couldn't be sure what we were seeing, but it was the *Varsovien* all right. The first bits of her we saw were high in the sky, illumined by lightning, and they might almost have been patches of silver sky. I instantly assumed that she was a long, tall ship stood on end, and I wondered how she had stayed upright for thousands of years, or however long it had been. A moment or two later, as we pulled into her wind-shadow, I realized how wrong I was. This was a ship. She lay on her side all right, but what a side! I was reminded of the Caradoc battlewagon I had seen high in the sky over Pharos. Beside this ship, the Caradoc carrier seemed like one of her own tiny helicopters. With the weather on Mormyr what it was, there was no way to see her whole, in all her glory. It would take hours to walk around her. She was five times as broad as any ship I had ever seen was high. She was built to carry a city inside her—a city with all its suburbs and its sources of supply. This ship was a world in her own right. Capable of swallowing moons? Easily, if she could open her mouth.

Eve took the maiden closer, until she was under the curve of the ship's belly. For the first time, we were all but out of the storm. Only a rare freak gust threw a handful of raindrops in to patter against the maiden's hull. We continued to drive along her length, slowly, searching for a blemish in the skin that was still highly polished despite centuries of corrosion.

"Any idea how we're supposed to get in?" I asked Ecdyon.

"If we find a lock," he said, "I imagine that I can open it."

"You were maybe expecting something this size?" I asked him.

"No," he replied, making that odd blinking gesture with his eyes—the only attempt at a change of expression he'd been able to adopt for use in conversation with humans. As it served all purposes, it wasn't too communicative, but I thought this time he was merely trying to confirm his denial—to underline it, as if to say *"Nobody* could have expected this."

"You realize that it's futile," I said, not only to Maslax, but to Ecdyon as well. "This whole thing has been a wild-goose chase. From the moment Stylaster contacted Charlot, this thing has been an utter and complete farce. Just take a look at this thing. It was never intended to come within a thousand miles of planetfall. She was built in orbit, and she was intended to stay in space. You can't *land* a thing like this. The power needed to land and take off would be absolutely impossible to generate, let alone control. This thing is down here for good, believe you me. *It'll never get off the ground.* Whoever dumped it might just as well have sent it cruising into the sun."

"You'd better be wrong," said Maslax.

"No. *You're* wrong. Can't you see that? Can't you see that you *have* to be wrong? This isn't a warship. It's not a

weapon. How could it be? Who'd build a weapon big
enough to house the population of a small world? Who'd
need a thing like this to fight a battle? Don't be a fool.
There's only one thing that any people could want a ship
like this for. Only one. The only thing one could possibly
want that much *space* for is *people.* This is a *migration*
ship, don't you see? It's an intergalactic. Hell, I don't
know what the bloody thing is doing *here,* of all places. I
can think of no reason whatsoever why the Gallacellans
would willingly abandon such a ship. But all you have to
do is *look,* man! Can you really sit there and tell me that's
a weapon? Can you?"

"The ship is armed," said Maslax.

"The ship is *dead,*" I said. "Stone dead. We've all been
wasting our time. We've all been wrong. Dead wrong. I
thought this was a warship they'd hidden away just in case
they ever wanted to change their minds. But it's not. It
can't be."

"I can see a hatch," said Eve.

"Can we reach it?" I asked. At first I couldn't see it.
Then I spotted it, well under the belly. It was high above
us, but in the shelter of the ship we could erect a ladder
from the maiden. If Ecdyon could get us inside, then we
could see for ourselves what kind of ship it was.

Eve drew to a halt, and commented: "It's a good thing
we found it when we did."

"Why?" asked Maslax.

She pointed. There was no way of knowing how much
of the *Varsovien* there there still was, extending into the
fog and the rain, but there was no doubt at all that the
rest would not be easy to get to. Ten yards in front of
us, there was a dip in the ground, and the shelf of rock
along which we had been driving came to an abrupt end.
Beyond the lip of the rock was swamp. Beyond that,
probably the sea.

8

Ecdyon and I labored to extend a ladder to the port while Maslax held his gun on Eve in the privacy of the iron maiden. I was grateful for the opportunity to exchange a few words with Ecdyon, but the exchange revealed absolutely nothing. I told him that this was no time to be holding out, and that if he'd told me any lies he'd better amend them right away. Bearing in mind the desperate state of our situation, I expected him to tell me the truth. Perhaps he did.

He claimed, in fact, that he already had.

"Now look," I said. "This just does not make sense. You claim you know nothing except what Stylaster has told you. You did not know anything about this ship other than the fact—if it is a fact—that it was left here a thousand years ago? But you also didn't know that the Gallacellans had ever used weapons?"

"What I have said is what I know," he persisted.

"What about what you told Maslax? Do you have any idea what Stylaster intended to do once we brought him here? Could you lift the ship, if it could be lifted?"

"That was true as well."

"You're a great help," I told him. "So who told Maslax about the Fenris device?"

"There is no such thing," he said. His voice was difficult to catch because of the noise of the storm.

"Well," I said, "let's not be too sure of that. Your ignorance, it seems, is limitless. Suppose there is a Fenris device. Just suppose. Who told who?"

"I do not know. But . . ."

"That's what I wanted to hear," I said, as he paused. "Come on. Tell me the but."

"I do not know whether it is true. . . ."

"Tell me anyway."

"The hierarchy is not united on this matter. Stylaster has not the backing of many of the castes. We have no quarrels, you understand. We are a peaceful people. But there are people who might not want the *Varsovien* recovered. I do not know why. I have heard only rumors that this is so. There is a ship called the *Cicindel* . . ."

"The ship that wouldn't answer," I said, remembering. "In the system, heading toward the *Saberwing* after the mayday call."

"That is right. The *Cicindel* is rumored to represent other interests in this affair. It is from another system. It might have been sent to . . . observe . . . the progress of Stylaster's plan. The *Cicindel* has been in the system for some time. It has not come to Iniomi. But it has landed once. On Pallant."

"Now there's a thing," I said. "The Gallacellans have their little games to play as well."

It dawned on me then how unfair it was of me to expect Ecdyon to know all things Gallacellan. Did I have encyclopedic knowledge of human affairs? True, I could give a quick rundown of who was liable to play what dirty trick on who within the foreseeable future, but I was certainly not privy to the inside information—only to the rumors and the speculations. What would I tell an alien who asked about Caradoc's precise plans for furthering its commercial stranglehold on known space? What *could* I tell him? And Ecdyon, despite his association with Stylaster, was less likely to be in a position of omniscience than I, with my proximity to Charlot. I wanted to apologize to him, but I couldn't see how to do it without a lengthy explanation of why I was sorry. And the ladder was in position. There was no time.

I never did get to give Ecdyon that apology.

It didn't prove to be difficult to get into the *Varsovien*. Any child could have done it. The airlock was vast—it accommodated all four of us easily. Personally, I wasn't happy about all four of us boarding her. I would much rather Eve—and perhaps Ecdyon too—had stayed in the maiden. But Maslax reckoned to need them both— Ecdyon to help me sort out what was what, and Eve to hold as the hostage I would least like to see shot to pieces. We all came up the ladder, and we all entered the ship.

Beyond the lock there was a cylindrical chamber which appeared to have no other door save the lock itself. On the wall was a panel with a whole sequence of buttons. I say "wall" although the room was oriented at right angles to the natural direction of gravity—obviously the cylinder was supposed to be stood on end with a single circular wall. But the ship was laid on its side. We had to crouch down and crane our necks sideways to inspect the writing beside the buttons.

"What does it say?" I asked Ecdyon—then, with sudden doubt: "You can read, can't you?"

"I can read," he said. "This is an elevator shaft. One of the buttons is labeled 'control level.' Shall I press it?"

"Go ahead," said Maslax.

Ecdyon pressed one of the buttons. Nothing happened.

"It's all switched off," said Eve.

"Is there an activator button?" I asked the Gallacellan.

"This one here is marked only with a symbol," he said. "I do not understand the symbol. Shall I press it?"

"Might as well," I said. "If it isn't the activator it won't have any effect, will it?"

Ecdyon pressed the button, and we fell.

For once, I'd been thinking just half an instant ahead of my actions. Even as I told Ecdyon to press the button I was realizing that when the elevator was activated the artificial grav-field would come into play. Then down would very rapidly become sideways, and we would all end up in a heap on the tail-end of the cylindrical chamber.

As we fell, I was all ready to grab Maslax's gun and blast a hole in his left arm just below the elbow. It would have to be a real trick-shot, but with the wind to help me I thought I could pull it off. But I failed. Even as Maslax fell, his hand clutched more tightly around the gun. He hadn't taken his finger away from the stud. It went off.

I was already reaching for him, but in the split second while his hand convulsed, the wind realized what was happening, and I snatched my hand away. The beam barely touched the gauntlet of my suit, and didn't do any real damage.

Ecdyon was not so lucky. He intercepted the beam with his upper torso.

Maslax relaxed his grip almost instantly, and the beam cut out. The suit gave the Gallacellan a lot of protection, and it no doubt saved his life, but he was literally writhing in pain on the floor. His flailing limbs caught me in the midriff and threw me backward, robbing me of all the thin hope I retained of being able to disarm Maslax in the confusion. Eve was already crumpled up against the wall.

Maslax was the first to his feet. He was almost screaming.

"You should have warned me," he whined, and the note of hysteria was starkly clear in his voice. "That was *your* fault. I didn't mean to shoot him. I didn't!"

I knelt over Ecdyon, trying to get some idea of the damage. The wound on his flesh was blue-black, but so far as I could see there was little leakage of blood (I presumed Gallacellans had blood). He stopped writhing within the minute, and sounds came out of his hind mouth. He was trying to talk, but nothing was getting through except clicks and whistles, as though he couldn't make up his mind whether to groan in Gallacellan or in English.

Eventually—in a matter of minutes—he quieted. I peered through the visor of his suit, and I saw him deliberately blink his eyes.

"He's alive," said Maslax, still with the high-pitched tone in his voice. "I didn't kill him."

"Are you sure you have the guts to murder twenty-five million people at one stroke?" I asked him sourly, as Eve knelt to help me get Ecdyon to his feet.

Ecdyon tried to say something. It came out garbled, but English.

"Say again," I said to him, gently.

"I said: the air is . . ." He didn't manage to finish. But I nodded to signal that I got his meaning. The air was good. The hole in his suit hadn't done for him.

"We'd better not . . ." I began, intending to say that we had better not take off our helmets because Gallacellan air, though enough like ours to be breathable, wasn't ideal, and we had plenty of spare in the maiden. Then I thought better of it. Sometime or other, I was going to have to persuade Maslax to take off his suit so I could at least see the bomb trigger.

I started again: "We'd better not waste our own supplies," I said. "Close off the bottles and take off your helmets."

We all exposed our faces to the atmosphere. "A thousand years old," I murmured, "and still as fresh as they left it." It felt fresher to human senses than it really was, owing to traces of carbohydrate that were enough to register a scent, but quite harmless. There was a shade too much oxygen in it, which might have a mildly intoxicating effect, but I didn't mention it—there was no point in alerting Maslax to the fact.

"Which button do I press?" demanded Maslax, now returned to his customary harsh and hoarse tones.

Ecdyon reached out and pressed it for him. He whispered, "I'm all right." But I kept hold of his arms. He was heavy, and if he were to become a dead weight I probably couldn't hold him up. But I could give him a little assistance in standing.

The elevator went up. I remembered that we were now traveling *along* the ship, out into the swamplands.

The journey seemed to take an age, though it was only

two or three minutes. There were no flashing lights on the panel to show our progress.

When we stopped, the room revolved slowly so that the door was now oriented in the opposite direction. It still had to be opened manually. There was another door beyond it, and when we had passed through that one we found ourselves in another elevator. The only difference so far as I could see was in the pattern of the buttons on the control panel. These were arranged in a square rather than a column.

Ecdyon leaned over to read all the labels.

"Where do we want to go?" he asked.

"The control room," I said.

"There is no control room," he said.

"This is the control level."

"Yes."

"Then there must be a control room."

"No. Virtually all these labels refer only to repair facilities. There is only an observation room and a monitoring room. No reference to controls at all, in the sense that you mean."

"What other sense?" I asked quickly.

"I cannot tell," he said, "but there is something about these buttons which implies that the ship is completely automatic."

"That's not very practical," I said. "Even if it uses only a robot pilot there has to be some provision for programming a flight plan."

"There is no button," said Ecdyon.

"Get on with it," said Maslax.

"It's all very well for you to say get on with it," I told him. "Suppose *you* choose. Pick a button . . . any button."

But Ecdyon cut short any argument that might have developed by reachng out a large finger and pushing one. We began to move again—not up or down, but sideways. The trip this time was much shorter. Only a matter of seconds.

Again, we found a double door giving us access into another chamber with only the one entrance/exit. This one was much larger, though, and it certainly wasn't an elevator. I didn't have to ask which button Ecdyon had selected. This was the observation room. There was a row of couches, and a plinth in the center of the room on which were mounted more buttons—presumably to control the screen.

I didn't wait for Maslax to object. I lurched forward with Ecdyon, and with some help from Eve I managed to get him into a reasonable coil on one of the softly cushioned couches. He spread himself into a much flatter coil than the one I'd seen him adopt previously, and he looked more like a python than ever.

"Do you want to get out of the suit?" I asked him, as I placed both our helmets on the next couch.

"Please," he said, "a moment of rest first."

Maslax was standing back in the doorway, looking around. Eve, having put down her own helmet, went forward to the plinth and punched a button. The lights went out. Maslax had hardly begun to frame a wordless cry of anger when she contrived to reverse the process and said, "Sorry."

The next button she pressed brought the screen to life. It hummed very faintly for a few seconds, then stopped as an image appeared in glorious technicolor. It came as no surprise to find that we were looking out into the atmosphere of Mormyr. Presumably, we had a view from the bow of the ship, because all we could see was storm and sea. The water was dark and ugly, lashed into a fury by wind and rain, bubbling and hissing like boiling milk. The hissing, of course, was suggested rather than heard. It was silent as a tomb so far inside the *Varsovien*. In the outer lift shaft, we had been able to hear the clatter of the hail against the outer hull transmitted through the metal, but that noise had been slowly muffled as we moved into the heart of the ship, and now, with the door of the observation room having been closed by Maslax, there was no sound at all.

"Not very interesting," I commented.

"Shall I try for a different picture?" asked Eve, studying the other buttons ruminatively.

"No," said Maslax. "Let's go."

"Where to?" I asked.

"He mentioned a monitoring place," said Maslax, pointing at Ecdyon with the flopping gauntlet at the end of his left arm. As the limp material of the suit moved I could see the outline of the triggering device, held in his left hand.

"He's hurt," I said. "He can't go traipsing all over the ship. Can't we leave him here?"

"No," Maslax said abruptly. There was no real need for an explanation. Only Ecdyon could read Gallacellan.

Only . . .? I suddenly thought, as I remembered the passenger in my mind. Hey, I said silently. Can you read?

—Naturally, he said.

You might mention these things, I rebuked him.

—I took it for granted . . . he began.

Hell! I said, suddenly—almost aloud as a new thought struck me. I bet you can speak it too. You can talk Gallacellan.

—Well, he said, I don't know about that. I can *understand* Gallacellan, though the language has . . . matured . . . a little in a thousand years plus. But whether I can *speak* it—I mean, with your vocal cords. That's another matter.

I hesitated. Should I tell Maslax I could do my own navigating? I decided there was no point. He probably wouldn't leave Ecdyon loose in the ship anyway.

Back into the elevator we all went, and off we went again, this time to the monitoring room. I had a sneaking suspicion that this might be it. If one one were going to hide a manual control panel anywhere, the logical place to do it would have to be the place where one had the facilities to monitor all the ship's instruments and mechanical devices. I expected to find the monitoring room a veritable maze of machinery and instrumentation.

In actual fact, it was surprisingly sparse. There was a console running around the room about four feet from the ground, but it was only a foot deep and it wasn't a very big room. There couldn't have been more than a couple of hundred information outputs, and most of them were tape-clutches, screens, and speakers rather than dials. On the far wall, however, above the console, was a single panel with a big switch set in it.

Ecdyon stepped forward to precede the rest of us into the room, and he supported himself against the console while he began to read the manifold labels and signs that were all over the panels of the console.

Maslax, though, had eyes for one thing only. As he stepped past me I turned to look at him.

"Is that the activator switch?" he asked Ecdyon.

The Gallacellan looked up, saw where Maslax was pointing, and said. "I think so. . . ."

I watched Maslax put the gun between his teeth and reach up to the big switch on the wall. I spent a couple of valuable seconds inwardly wondering whether I could jump him while he had the gun in his teeth, and then the full import of what he was doing dawned on me.

"Oh God no!" I yelled. *"Don't touch it!"*

I plunged forward, but he mistook my action and yanked the switch down hard, then snatched the gun from his teeth to ram it hard into my chest. He didn't fire, but for one horrible moment I almost wished that he had.

Into the silence of the room surged a deep-throated murmur that grew and grew. I almost imagined the room shuddering, but all was absolutely and perfectly still. There was just the deep, deep noise hammering at my ears. The entire console seemed to spring to life as tapes chattered, screens lit up, and the needles of such dials as there were leaped from the null position.

Maslax looked scared. His face was paper-white. "What's happening?" he wanted to know.

"You stupid bloody fool!" I howled at him, with the gun still jammed hard into my fifth rib. "This is an automatic ship! she's already programmed. Don't you see?"

"She's *lifting!*"

9

He stood there looking at me, for just a moment, looking as if things were utterly and totally beyond him. Uncertain, frightened, childlike.

Then he smiled.

I think I'd rather have seen the gorgon smile than watch that slow grin spread spread across his warped little face.

"That's right," he said. "That's all right. I knew we could do it. You see, this is what I wanted. You see?"

I was rendered almost speechless. I just shook my head, and said—in a perfectly level, ordinary tone of voice— "The storm will break us into a million little pieces. She just isn't built for it. There's no ship in the known galaxy that could do it. No ship."

But Ecdyon had been reading the labels all around the room. "I think you're wrong," he said. "You said that the ship was never intended to take off. But right here, on this screen, there is a series of ... words, symbols, I cannot read all of it. But it is a program for takeoff. The ship was left ready to lift. It was built for it."

I knew that he was right and I was wrong. I could feel it, in the deep, heavy throb of the ship as she mustered her forces, distributed them, and put them into action. I had been too free with my impossibles. Once again I had misjudged the limits of my own ignorance. The Gallacellans, it seemed, were capable of a lot more than I'd ever given them credit for.

While I was busy lamenting my mistakes, Eve picked out the really important thought and exposed it for us all to see.

"Johnny and the captain," she said softly. "They're still down there. They've no way back."

Maslax looked me in the eye, but he couldn't hold the stare. His gaze dropped.

"You can go back," he said. "You can take the ship back down. You can go get them. But not until we've been to Pallant. Not until we've used the Fenris device."

I felt quite helpless. I had been riding the tide of events for a long time, and now it had taken me too far. At last, the situation was rendered impossible. I was left alone with the consequences of my own inaction.

Eve, a madman, a wounded Gallacellan, and a gigantic ship bound for an unknown destination. Probably Andromeda. I felt at that moment as though Andromeda was a pretty fitting destination. Right out of this world. Out of the known galaxy, out of the whole damn galaxy altogether. Into the mighty dark. We'd all be dead, of course. It was a long way to Andromeda.

"Maslax," I said quietly, "the *Varsovien* is already programmed. It's not going to Pallant. We don't know where it's going. You've killed us, Maslax. You, Eve, Ecdyon, me—we're all dead, just as dead as if you'd pulled that trigger. And the *Hooded Swan*. What use is the bomb to you now, Maslax? That ship is already doomed. Blowing it now would only be a mercy killing."

Eve took my arm. "Stop it, Grainger," she said. "There's no need for that. There must be a way to override the controls—to reprogram the ship. We must be able to take control of the ship."

"What for?" I said, spreading my arms wide in a gesture of bitterness and defeat. "So that crazy cripple can tell us to go murder Pallant? So he can shoot us all down when we refuse? How do we win, Miss Lapthorn? You tell me that—just how do we win? We're trapped between the devil and the mighty dark. There's no way. No way at all."

—She's right, said the wind. This is no time for you to indulge your penchant for self-pity. There must be a reprogramming inlet if there isn't a manual override. We have to find it. First, though, we have to take Maslax.

It was a remarkably sane and sensible summation of the situation. I wasn't feeling too sane and sensible just at that moment, but I had to admit that when I finally did get around to thinking about it, that would definitely be the way the cookie had crumbled.

At that moment, though, there were other thoughts dancing in my mind. Like, for one, this ship was rising steadily through the worst conditions any spaceship had ever survived. Sure, she was big and strong, but could she do it? I wished that I was back in the screen room so that I could watch the fiery sky until it disappeared and left us alone with black infinity and stars. Even if we made it out of atmosphere, could we ever come back? Logic said yes—somebody has sent the *Varsovien* down to Mormyr in the first place—but fear said no.

I needed somewhere to sit down, but there probably wasn't a chair in the entire ship. Only those damned coiling-couches. And there weren't even those in here.

The long silence gave Maslax a chance to decide that he was still in command of the situation, still handing out the orders.

"You," he said, indicating Ecdyon, "you read the screens and things. Figure out how to make this thing go where we want it to. You two just stand still."

"Can I take my suit off?" I asked. I was hoping, of course, for a general disrobing. Maslax nodded, and I began to strip the suit off. Eve followed my example, but Maslax showed no sign of doing the same, and when Ecdyon paused, the little man told him to get on with his allotted task. I could see that the Gallacellan was still supporting himself by leaning on the console, but there was no way to find out how badly he was injured. Probably he couldn't tell himself.

"And while you're at it," added Maslax. "Find out how to operate the Fenris device."

I was sick to death of that damned Fenris device. Who had called it that? Not a Gallacellan, obviously. Ferrier? But who was Ferrier? And why had the Gallacellans in the *Cicindel* contacted him?

"You won't accept it, will you?" I said to him. "There is no Fenris device. Why would anyone put a weapon like that on to a ship that's obviously built for carrying people?"

"There *is* a Fenris device," he said coldly.

"So OK," I said, feeling that the time had finally come to insist that some of this mess was sorted out. "You help us to find it. You tell us what you know. Just tell us how you found out about the bloody thing and what you think it is."

He licked his lips.

"I read it," he said.

"In a book of fairy tales?" I suggested.

"In his *mind!*"

"Whose mind?"

"Ferrier's. Ferrier knew. They told him—the Gallacellans. They sent him a message. . . ."

"Which you read?" I guessed.

"I read his *mind,*" insisted Maslax.

"OK," I said. "You read his mind. So what did the message say?"

"It said that the ship on Mormyr that Titus Charlot was trying to raise was armed with a weapon that could eat up moons, and Ferrier laughed when he told told that woman, and she . . . He said it was a Fenris device, and he laughed. They both laughed because they didn't understand, and they thought it was a joke. The message said that Ferrier ought to stop Titus Charlot, for everyone's sake, because Stylaster didn't know what was best for either humans or Gallacellans. And Ferrier laughed because he thought it was a joke, and the woman, she . . ."

Maslax's voice petered off again. He couldn't seem to remember what the woman had done.

I didn't understand. Ferrier was a big man—that we had been told. But there was nobody on Pallant big enough to put in a polite request to Titus Charlot, let alone tell him what to do. Who was Ferrier—the law? Was he, after all, a king?

Eve, apparently moved by a sudden insight or inspiration, said: "What did the woman do? What did she do to make you kill them? What happened next? After you heard him read the message to her?"

Maslax's eyes narrowed.

"I had a reason," he said, harking back to our earlier conversation. "I had to kill them. I had no choice. You don't understand. You don't know what it was like. You just can't understand . . ."

"Tell us," said Eve, pressing home her advantage. "Make us understand. Tell us what it was like."

I'd already tried that, but I guess I just didn't have Eve's diplomatic touch. This time, it set him off. This time, he began to make us understand.

"They hate me," he said. "They always hated me. I only had to walk down the street, and everyone I passed —everyone—looked down at me—they always look *down*—and I'd hear them, inside their heads. I'd see it there, in their faces. As soon as I could read I could read it in their minds—animal—ugly—cripple—goblin—hate and fear, whenever eyes looked at me. And even when they wouldn't look—couldn't look—they'd be peeping and I could read the words—hideous—creature— dwarf—miserable—always the same. Everyone I passed on the street. Other children—used to try to kill me—used to laugh and chase and hurt. When I got a job—with machines, machines don't think, don't hate, don't fear, don't use the words—it went on. I was bad with machines—big hands—clumsy. They wouldn't let me be with the machines—fetch and carry—sweep up—lift this—take this message. They wouldn't let me have a job—not with the machines—not even the typers—big fingers—slow—fetch and carry. And every day—all of them—send him away—make him work somewhere else—don't want him here—ugly—little—creature—insect—spider—foul—go away—sweep up—in the cellar. When they spoke—their voices—talk down, talk sweet—patient—nice—friendly —inside, hate and fear—loathing—despising—revulsion—read the minds, not hear the words—call me surly—sullen—vile—hate me—hate me. Years and years—they don't know that I can hear them, read their minds. They don't know that I can see the words, that I know, that I understand. They think they have me fooled. They think Maslax—some kind of insect—little—mad—stupid—feeble-minded. But it's not true. I can read. I know them. I know just what they are. No more than the machines they work—less—every day those machines print out things they want to know—thousands of pages—everything—the machines know—the people, they know *nothing*. Nothing but what the machines say. They think they're everything, but they're not. They can't even read . . ."

"This place where you worked," I interjected, as softly as I could. "What was it?"

He had been flickering his eyes back and forth from the ceiling to Eve to the floor to Eve . . . Now he stopped and looked at me.

"It was the Library," he said.

And there it was—the vital piece. It was all in place. I knew what had happened now.

"Go on," Eve prompted the little man. "What happened before you killed Ferrier?"

"Ferrier," he said, rolling the name around on his tongue as if he wanted to spit it out. "Ferrier was the boss. The big man. Always peering—walking—inspecting. Couldn't stand the sight of me. Wanted to be rid of me. But he couldn't—not on Pallant—everybody works on Pallant. Made me do work over again—swore at me— laughed at me. *He* didn't care if I knew he hated me. He *liked* hating me. He *liked* letting me know. I could read him—vicious. He had a woman—working on the machines—used to come to see her—meet her. She hated me too—he made her hate me more—they talk about me—laugh—swear—he hurt me for *her*. I read her mind—hideous—nasty—horrid—brute—beast—spider. They *say* those things. They don't know I can hear. But I'm always there—I'm always around. Out of sight—they all want me out of sight. I help them—I have my hiding holes—I have my places. Out of sight—I can hear what they say. I can read what they think. I hear them when they get the message. They laugh and laugh loud—they don't understand—they're happy—they kiss and they say good-bye for now. The woman, she comes out of the office. Too sudden. I am in the corridor, she bumps me, she falls. A filing cabinet is open—the drawer has a sharp edge. She is cut, not bad, just on her arm. It bleeds—lot of blood—not bad, but she screams and she screams. More at me than because she is hurt. Ferrier comes out. He yells at me, he kicks me, she is still screaming, still bleeding. He says he's going to kill me—I know he doesn't mean it, but he comes after me when I run and I keep running. I run right away, but only to my hiding place. Then I get my gun, I come back, and I kill them both. They scream again, and they keep screaming. They are dead—I killed them—but their minds—I can read their minds. Their minds keep on screaming. The words—I can still read the words—they keep coming out—filthy—beast—vermin—kill it. . . ."

He stopped.

"OK," I said. "We know the rest."

There was a gap of some several minutes while he replayed all the things he's said to us through his mind. I didn't have to be a mind reader to know he was doing that. Any more than he had to be a mind reader to know what people thought when they passed him on the street or told him to get out of sight. Maybe he'd missed reading one or two words of pity, maybe a little sympathy here and there, certainly a lot of indifference. But one could hardly say that what he'd picked up was completely false and imagined. He didn't have to read minds. He knew all right.

I turned to Eve. "It's all a tragic mistake," I told her. "It's a misunderstanding. Difficulties in translation. The Gallacellans didn't want to know about humans—they never wanted to know. Only a handful, like Ecdyon, knew anything about us. And they're under obligation, you see—Ecdyon works for Stylaster. Stylaster regards him as an extra leg, or a sense-organ, or something. What Ecdyon knows, Stylaster knows. But it couldn't possibly occur to another Gallacellan to come to Ecdyon or to anyone like him and *ask* him about humans. Status, you see. The Gallacellans just didn't understand."

"What are you talking about?" she asked.

"This whole crazy affair. Can't you see what's been happening? Stylaster wants to raise the *Varsovien*. He has to use our ship, but *using* us is exactly what he tries to do. It would no more occur to him to give away one extra fact than it would occur to the Caradoc Company to finance the Library at New Alexandria. Stylaster uses Charlot. Some other Gallacellan wants to let sleeping dogs lie, wants to let the *Varsovien* stay exactly where she is. How does he go about doing it? Does he go to Charlot? Of course not. Automatic Gallacellan policy is to go to the man of higher status."

"But Charlot has no superiors," she said.

"Exactly. But do *they* know that? What do they know about Charlot? Nothing. Or next to nothing. What can they find out about him? Without violating status, next to nothing. They know he's a big man in the Library. Obviously, they want to contact the top man in the Library. But they don't know the difference between New Alexandria and the tinpot data collation agency on Pallant. They send the message to Ferrier—one of the most absurd cases of mistaken identity on record, but given the Gallacellan methods, quite plausible. Ferrier, of course, thinks it's a joke. He reads it out to his office staff. There's some phrase about destroying moons—maybe the message isn't so very good English—and Ferrier shows off how erudite and witty he is by making that crack about the Fenris device. But Maslax is eavesdropping, and he doesn't see the joke. Minutes later, the joke turns sour. And here we are. Dead meat, the lot of us. All because of a bloody silly mistake."

"I wasn't eavesdropping," said Maslax.

"No," I said, with tired sarcasm, "you were reading the letter through Ferrier's eyes by sheer power of mind. Great stuff. But if you read my mind now you'll find that I've had just about enough. Why don't you give me the gun and the bomb-trigger and let's all pack it in and go home?"

He wasn't impressed. He was still determined to send the entire population of Pallant to keep Ferrier and his girlfriend company in the fires of Hell.

"Mr. Grainger," said Ecdyon, interrupting. "There's a ship trying to contact us."

"The *Cicindel?*"

"I think it's the ship from Pallant. *The Gray Goose.*"

"You'd better ..." I began. But all this going over Maslax's head seemed to have upset him a little.

"*I'll* talk to them," he said. "You just keep quiet. Grainger, if you open your mouth I'll blast you. Now just keep quiet. You—let's hear what they want to say."

Ecdyon fiddled with the controls, and then stepped back. As he moved, he staggered slightly.

There was a moment's silence. Then we heard the man on the *Gray Goose* begin a standard call signal. He addressed us as "the ship out of Leucifer V" and reeled off his identification codes. Then he paused and waited. I heard a muffled sound as he said something to one of his fellows—he was probably wondering if we could hear him.

"Can you hear me?" said Maslax, tentatively.

"Hello?" said the other. "Hello? Are you aboard the vessel from Leucifer V? Please identify yourself."

"This is Maslax," said Maslax. He had a keen sense of melodrama but no sense of propriety.

"Who is in command of this vessel?" asked the policeman.

"I'm in command," said Maslax. "This vessel is under

my orders." He sounded oddly calm and proud. He knew
that only his voice was reaching the police ship. They
couldn't see him. They had only his voice and what he
said by which to judge him. If his voice was calm and
strong and proud, then so was he as his voice went out on
the circuit into space. This was his moment, and he knew
it.

"What ship are you?" asked the policeman. "Identify
yourself."

"This is the *Varsovien*," said Maslax. The statement
had a majestic simplicity that authorized identification
procedure seems to lack.

"You are ordered to surrender yourself and your ship,"
said the other, after a brief pause for a whispered consultation. "You are under arrest. We intend to board you."

Just at that moment, the deep note of the *Varsovien's*
drive changed. It was a very subtle change, and only a
pilot would have noticed it. I did. Eve did. We exchanged a
glance. We were building up to tachyonic transfer. We
were going to go transcee.

"If you come any closer," said Maslax, who was still
relishing his role as Captain Blood, "then we shall open
fire and destroy you."

There was another muttered consultation aboard the
Gray Goose.

"What do you intend to do?" asked the policeman. I
had been hoping that he wouldn't ask that. He wasn't
going to like the answer.

"The *Varsovien* is bound for Pallant," said Maslax,
which was a blatant lie, because we didn't even know
which direction we were headed. "We intend to annihilate
all human life on the planet."

The whispered conversation seemed to get heated.

They had to make a decision on the spur of the moment. It was a tough decision. I hoped against hope that
they weren't going to be silly, but I was hoping against the
odds. Cops are cops.

"Our instruments show that you will make transfer in
about one and a half minutes," said the policeman. "We'll

give you just one minute. If you don't slow down within that time and acknowledge that we may board you, then we will fire on you."

Maslax looked at Ecdyon.

"Destroy that ship," he ordered.

"No," said Ecdyon.

"I order you to fire on that ship," Maslax repeated, tight-lipped. He was still playing his role.

"No," said Ecdyon.

"He's a Gallacellan, Maslax," I said. "He could no more fire on that ship than you could destroy it by spitting at it. It's just not in him to do it."

Seconds were ticking by.

Maslax turned his attention to me, but he pointed the gun at Eve.

"Then you do it," he said.

"I don't know how," I told him.

"The alien will tell you how. You will fire on that ship."

I shook my head. "No I won't," I said.

"You'll fire," he repeated. "Quickly. If you don't, I'll kill the woman."

I just kept shaking my head. "I'm not going to do it," I said. "You have the gun, you've had it all along the line. You've always been able to shoot. You still can. But it won't do you any good at all. I'm not going to fire on . . ."

We heard—but did not feel—the impact of a missile somewhere in the bowels of the ship. I heard the distant sound of bells, and the muffled grating of machinery coming into operation. The note of the drive changed again. The automatics had changed their mind about transfer. We were decelerating again.

". . . that ship," I finished.

We all looked around a little furtively, as if unsure that we had a right to be still alive. But of course we were still alive. The *Gray Goose* was an ant and we were a whale. We hardly felt the bite. It was a nuisance, an inconvenience, but it wasn't going to do any substantial damage.

"I don't think they should have done that," I remarked.

Meanwhile, aboard the *Gray Goose,* they had noticed our deceleration. They took it as a sign of our capitulation.

"Calling *Varsovien,*" said the voice. "We are approaching. Don't try anything or we'll blast you again. We intend to board you and we advise you to surrender."

"Shut it off," said Maslax to Ecdyon. The Gallacellan made no move, and Maslax repeated the command, his voice getting nastier. Ecdyon complied.

The dwarf returned his attention to me. "Destroy that ship," he said, yet again.

"No," I said, patiently and firmly.

"If you don't destroy the *Gray Goose,*" he said, "then I'm going to destroy the *Hooded Swan*. He raised his left arm. The half-empty gauntlet on the end dangled its fingers in the most absurd manner.

I'd known, of course, that it had to come to this eventually. I'd already made up my mind what to do—not that there was any real question about it. There was no threat in the world could make me fire on the *Gray Goose* or anyone else.

"Maslax," I said levelly, "you have already destroyed the *Hooded Swan*. When you activated this ship and lifted from Mormyr, you destroyed the *Hooded Swan* as surely as if you had triggered that bomb. There's only you and us, Maslax, that's all. You have the gun. But I'm not going to fire on that ship, nor is Eve, nor is Ecdyon. Nor are we going to tell you how. Any destruction you have thoughts of carrying out is going to take place right here in this room. No one is going to shoot down the *Gray Goose,* much less is anyone going to fire a shot at Pallant. There's nothing you can do, Maslax. Nothing at all. Except shoot the three of us, with that one little gun. And even then, you might not get us all. You've nothing left, Maslax, nothing at all."

I almost wished for a moment that he could really read minds. Because then he'd know that I meant it.

Maslax hesitated.

"We're changing course," said Ecdyon, anxious to take some of the tension out of the showdown.

"Why?" I asked, keen to help him. Maslax was still wavering.

"I think we're turning away from the groove that the *Gray Goose* is coming in on," he said.

Presumably we were programmed to take evasive action after having been fired upon.

"Better hear what the *Gray Goose* thinks about that," I said. Ecdyon turned the call circuit back on.

We just had time to hear them threatening to fire before Maslax howled "No!" and hurled himself on Ecdyon. Ecdyon towered above the tiny man, but the impetus of Maslax's leap knocked him sideways against the panel and obviously brought a wave of pain from his wound. Ecdyon crumpled up and Maslax ran his hand randomly over the switches. The policeman's voice cut out abruptly.

I went to help Ecdyon, while Maslax leaned against the instruments, uncertain where to point the gun, uncertain whether to shoot and who to shoot at if he did. He was angry, and frustrated, but he was scared as well. He had lost control of the situation, his fantasies of a colossal revenge had been dissolved. He was helpless, despite the fact that he still had the gun and the bomb. He just didn't know what to do. There wasn't anything he *could* do, except take it out on us. He wasn't going to do that, because we were all the audience he had. We were all the people there were who had seen that Maslax wasn't just a crawling insect, wasn't just a butt for everyone's laughter, a repository for all their spare hatred. We were the only people who could testify to his real power and his real existence.

I knew he wouldn't kill us then. Not all of us at once. He needed company more than he needed corpses. When it came to the last act—the final corner—well, that was a different matter. Then he'd shoot. He'd shoot and he'd keep on shooting till they got him. But not yet. We had time, if nothing else.

There was the dull sound of another impact, and I

guessed that the *Gray Goose* had opened fire again. If in
doubt, shoot it out. Stupid bastard cops, I thought. I
helped Ecdyon rise to his feet again. He was weak; I had
to take a lot of his weight. He was hurt badly. The lips of
his foremouth were writhing helplessly, and I could see the
rows of teeth inside—grinding teeth, not sharp, cutting
teeth.

There were long minutes when he didn't look at the instruments, when Maslax came away from the wall and
backed up toward the door as Eve moved in to see if she
could help. For those few moments, Ecdyon was occupied
solely with himself.

When he looked back again at the panel where he'd
been attending to the call circuit and following the course
of events he made a sudden, sharp noise like a cat cough-
ing, and then a sibilant whisper that sounded like a groan.
I thought it was his injuries, but I was wrong.

"The . . . ship . . ." he said painfully.

We waited.

"The . . . other ship," he said. "It's gone."

"What do you mean—gone?" I asked him, though I
knew very well what "gone" meant.

"It's not there," he said. "There's not even the dust.
Not an atom. Gone completely, disintegrated. There's a
sphere surrounding the ship. A sphere in which *nothing*
exists. Its radius is nearly five hundred thousand miles.
We're still moving. Even the dust—it's just disappearing.

"The Fenris device . . . it's on."

10

The switches," said Eve. "When he hit the switches with
his fist and the caller cut out. He must have switched it on
then."

"No," said Ecdyon. "There is no such switch. Not
there. All he did was switch off the call circuit. The sphere
had nothing to do with that."

"It must have come on automatically," I said. "When
the second missile hit us. The first teed it up. The second
set it off. It's independently programmed, just like everything else aboard this damned ship."

Maslax was only just coming around to realizing what
had happened.

"The *Gray Goose*," he said. "It's dead?"

"Not an atom left," I said, feeling quite sick at the
thought.

"I did it," he said. "I did it. I killed them. I showed
them what I can do, didn't I? They'll be sorry they ever
. . ."

"They'll be sorry, all right," I cut him off. "But there's
nothing left of them to show it. You didn't do it, you stupid little bastard. It was the ship."

It was risky, I suppose, calling him names like that. But
I felt like it.

"I did it," said Maslax.

"If he wants to think he did it," Eve said to me, "you'd better let him think he did it. No point in provoking him."

"He didn't have anything against them," I said. "What did they ever do to him?"

"They shot at us," said Eve.

"Honi soit qui mal y pense," I quoted, with savage sarcasm. I still remembered what happened to the last ships that shot at me. Their own missiles had set in process a reaction which destroyed them. I hadn't been sorry then—not in the least. But this didn't seem quite the same, somehow. Just an ant stinging a whale.

"I cannot tell," said Ecdyon, "but I think that there is nothing in our path, and we are traveling quite slowly."

"We aren't going to swallow any moons, then?" I asked.

"No moons," he said. Then: "Wait. The *Cicindel*—the other ship—it is behind us, coming on—they do not know—they cannot be aware. . . ."

He reached out for the switches that operated the call circuits, but Maslax jumped forward across the room and brought the butt of his gun hard down on the stretching fingers.

Ecdyon yelped, and I sagged under his weight as he swayed and transferred it from the console to my shoulder.

"No!" said Maslax. "Let them come!"

"Those are Gallacellans," I said. "That's the *Cicindel*—the ship which brought the message that sent you off on this crazy stunt. That's not a ship out of Pallant—the men on board it aren't even human. They're Gallacellans, damn it! You can't possibly have anything against them. They never hated you. They *couldn't* hate you. Your crazy ideas have nothing to do with them. You *can't* want them to be killed."

"Leave those switches alone," said Maslax.

"We have to warn that ship," I said. "They don't know what happened. They must think we fired on the *Gray Goose*. They're coming to investigate. They must know that this ship isn't in Gallacellan hands. They didn't want it brought up from Mormyr in the first place. *You must let us tell them not to come any closer."*

"No," he said. "You wouldn't blow up the *Gray Goose* for me. I won't save the *Cicindel* for you."

"I'm going to do it," I said. "You can shoot me if you like." I reached for the switches, realizing as I did so that I didn't know what to do, and turning my head toward Ecdyon, who had swayed back against the wall by now. While my head was turned, Maslax slammed the gun-butt down on my fingers just as he had on Ecdyon's.

It hurt. Had the console been flat and smooth he might have split the fingers, but as it was the panel sloped considerably and my fingers slipped between the switches. Nothing was broken and the skin was not cut. But I am inordinately sensitive about my fingers. I'm a pilot, and a pilot's life is in his fingertips. Even a bruise can mean the difference between life and death in a delicate balance in distorted space. I really wanted to clench my fist and knock Maslax across the room. I am not by nature a violent man but at that moment I felt close to murder. Self-control intervened, however, and I listened, instead, to what Maslax was saying.

"Touch those switches again," he threatened, "and I'll burn your hand off."

"How long?" Eve asked the Gallacellan.

"If neither ship changes speed," said Ecdyon, consulting the screens and the dials and calculating in his head, "I think about twenty minutes."

We had just twenty minutes to take Maslax, by force, by stealth, or by persuasion. Just twenty minutes, because I was determined that the *Cicindel* shouldn't follow the police boat to oblivion.

Come on, I said to the wind, think of something, damn you!

—You're bigger, you're faster, said the wind.

Not that way, I said. Not while he can press that trigger. There has to be another way. An easier way.

—There's only one other way.

Tell me.

—He's got a weak mind. He's mad. Break him.

I looked hard at the ugly, malevolent face of the little man. He was looking right back at me, and he was waiting—waiting with the gun, because he knew I was going to try something and he wanted to kill me. I could read it in his face—I didn't need telepathy. He actually wanted to give himself the pleasure of shooting me, and he was just waiting for me to give him the reason.

"What am I thinking, Maslax?" I rapped out. "Come on, tell me. Show me this mind reading talent of yours. Tell me what I'm thinking."

"Hate and fear," he said tautly. "Hate and fear."

I shook my head, and made every effort to sneer at him. "Wrong," I said. "That's wrong. I'm not afraid of *you*. I don't even hate you. Try again, Maslax. Tell me what I'm thinking. Give me the words. Come on, you read the words, don't you? There are words, up here, inside my head. Tell me what they are, Maslax. You can't read minds at all, can you? And you *know* it. I can take you Maslax, can't I? I can take you because you can't read my mind. You don't know what I'm going to do."

"I can read your mind," he said. But there was an edge in his voice. I was beginning to shake him. I'd picked out his weak spot. I was attacking his fantasies.

"Show me," I invited. "Give me the words. Come on, tell me. What are the words?"

"Cripple!" he said.

"Wrong."

"Hate—loathing—foul!"

"Wrong."

"Animal—insect—spider!"

"Wrong."

He screamed. *"You're lying!"*

"I'm not lying," I told him, keeping my voice level. "I'm not lying. You have the words wrong, Maslax. You can't read. But I don't want you to take my word for it. I'm going to prove it to you. I'm going to prove beyond every last vestige of doubt that you're wrong, and then you'll have to see it. Do you know how I'm going to do it?

You should, if you can read my mind. You should know exactly how I'm going to do it. Come on, Maslax, tell me. How am I going to prove you wrong? What am I going to do?"

I took a step forward, and he took a step back. He was frightened—really saturated with fear. I was astonished. Words, only words, but I had him moving backward. I had him retreating. The gun didn't matter: I had the weapon that mattered now—the only weapon that mattered. I took one more step forward and the stark terror in his eyes was a joy to behold.

"Come on," I said, my voice still quiet, but taking on a tone of calculated menace, "tell me. What am I going to do? I'm going to prove you wrong, aren't I? I'm going to prove to you that you can't read minds. And you *know* I'm going to prove it because you *don't know* what I'm going to do. Isn't that right? You know, don't you? You know I'm going to prove it."

I knew exactly what he was going to say and I was ready for him.

"You're not!" he squealed in anguish. "You're not because you *can't*. There's no way. There's nothing you can do. *Nothing!*"

"Nothing?" I said. "Nothing? Is that what I'm going to do? Nothing—because there's nothing I can do? Well, how about *this*, Maslax?"

And I took from the pocket of my jacket a pack of playing cards. I don't have many personal effects—I don't even wear a watch—but I do like to carry a pack of cards. Sometimes, I just turn them over, playing patience. It calms me after a flight. Sometimes, I seek out a game—a gambling game—because that soothes my nerves as well. Ever since Johnny took up gambling to pass away dead time on New Alexandria I'd been carrying this pack so that I could relieve him of a little of his pay now and again. With owing Charlot so much, I was always a little starved for cash.

Maslax looked at the pack of cards as if it were a rattlesnake about to bite him. He raised his gun and pointed it—not at me, but at the cards in my hand. He was afraid of those cards. He was afraid because he hadn't known they were there, and he was afraid because he knew what I was going to do with them.

"What's the matter, Maslax?" I asked him. "You can't be afraid of a little test of skill, now can you? You can read my mind, remember? There's nothing to be afraid of. Nothing at all. Here, I'll show you what we're going to do. I'll explain this little game we're going to play. I'm going to hold the pack in my hand, like this, so I can see the bottom card. I'm going to look at it hard, and concentrate on it. And then you're going to tell me what it is."

I riffled the cards once, and then held them up so that the card at the bottom was facing me. It was the seven of diamonds. I was just about to start, when it suddenly occurred to me that maybe—just maybe—I was wrong. Or maybe—just maybe—he would accidentally call the right card. It would only take once, just the first time, for the whole campaign to fall down. I riffled again, left fifty-one cards in my left hand, held between two fingers, and palmed one in my right hand. The one I palmed was the seven of diamonds—the facing card in the pack was now the jack of spades. It didn't matter now what card he called—I had one with which to prove him wrong.

"Call it," I said, holding the pack up in front of my face. "Call the card."

His mouth was open; he was staring. He was trying to speak, trying to force words out, but they wouldn't come. They wouldn't come because he was afraid.

"Come on, Maslax," I taunted. "You can do it. You can read my mind. Just tell me what the card is."

He went back one pace more, and would have gone two, but the wall stopped him; he was backed right up against it. He stammered, and he looked at the pack of cards the way people had been looking at him for years—or so he thought.

He finally got it out. "It's the jack," he said. "The jack of spades."

For a moment, my heart almost stopped beating.

I pretended to pull the card out, and produced the red seven from my right hand. I threw it at him, and he watched it flutter as if he were mesmerized by it. While he was watching it I shuffled the pack again and palmed another card—the three of diamonds—ready for a repeat performance. The seven settled face-up.

"There's your jack of spades," I said, loading all the mockery I could muster into my voice. "What's the next one? Come on, Maslax, *really* show us what you can do."

The new card facing me in the pack was the ten of hearts.

Maslax was breaking apart. "The jack," he said again. "It's the jack of *spades*."

I plucked the ten out of the pack and I let it fall, exposing it as I did.

"The next one, Maslax," I said. "Call the next one. Read my mind."

He moaned, and called the jack of spades for the third time. I turned the pack in my hand, still holding them. The bottom card was the six of clubs.

"Well," I said. "You don't seem to be able to read my mind after all."

He howled, and I threw the pack at the ceiling.

He fired, and the cards cascaded into a cloud of fire.

I dived forward, grabbed his left arm, and rammed the elbow back into the wall. I groped for the empty gauntlet, and felt the hard lump of the trigger device free of his nerveless, paralyzed fingers. Ecdyon, who had uncoiled into a long dive the moment I was out of the way, was grappling with the dwarf's gun hand, but it was no longer necessary. Maslax had crumpled up, and dropped the gun as if his right hand were as deadened as his left.

Eve picked it up.

We let him go, and turned back to the console where the screens still shone and the tape outlets ticked quietly away, dropping slow streamers onto the floor. A couple of smoldering cards clung to the console; the rest had fallen to the floor. I stamped out the remaining flames. There was a long dark scar on the ceiling where the beam had burned the plastic.

I felt weak. It was all I could do to stop my knees shaking. I'd piloted ships through the worst conditions imaginable, and I'd felt afterward as if I were fit to die. But I'd never felt quite like I felt then. It was only then that I realized that Maslax's naked fear had escalated at the same rate as my own deeply buried panic. When he called that first card correctly I had felt a wash of pure horror, but I had simply not recognized it. It suddenly struck me that I would never know whether Maslax had read my mind or not. I would never know whether I might not have beaten him by simply feeding him my own fear.

I shook my head, trying to clear it. "Call that ship," I said. "Warn them off."

I continued absorbing my state of tension, getting myself back into a state of calm, not paying any attention to what was going on around me now that all was well again. It was some moments before I realized that all was *not* well.

While those moments were wandering by, Eve was staring at me, and her realization that I wasn't aware was just as slow. Eventually she said, "Grainger," in a very low voice.

I looked at her, and then I looked where she was pointing.

Ecdyon had no sooner regained his feet after jumping Maslax than he had collapsed again. He was in an untidy sprawl all over the cabin floor. He was unconscious.

11

I realized that this was no time for standing around lamenting the cruelty of fate. I roused my languishing self-control.

"Get that suit off Maslax," I told Eve. "Let's have that little box of tricks of his in a safe place. I'll take care of this." I waved my hand perfunctorily to indicate that "this" covered everything to do with the instruments and switches.

OK, genius, I said—silently—so you can read. Anything he could do you can do better. Tell me which buttons to press and which knobs to turn.

—So you can do what? he asked.

So I can warn off the *Cicindel*. We'll get around to the next move after that's out of the way.

—How are you going to warn off the *Cicindel?* he wanted to know.

And was a good question.

You better teach me to click like a Gallacellan, fast, I said.

—No chance, he replied. You've got to let me have control. With full control, I just might—and I mean *might*—be able to produce some sound by which I can make myself understood. But I need that control. You must see that.

I saw it. But I didn't like it. Sure, he'd taken control before—once in the Halcyon Drift, once on Chao Phrya when his talents as a musician became desperately important. But the first time I was cradled and hooded, and the second time there was no one around who was in any fit condition to watch. This time was different. I was mobile, operative, and Eve was standing right behind me. It seemed somehow quite indecent to let someone else have my body and my voice when other people were not only watching but might actually want to exchange merry chitchat.

—Grainger, said the wind, we're running out of time.

There was, I knew, no alternative. There was no future at all in his producing click-patterns in my mind and my trying to duplicate them. But still I hesitated. If I was helpless, sure, I'd hand over automatically. But I didn't *feel* helpless. I was on my feet and moving.

—If you can't let go, he said, you'll have to let me knock you out.

But that was right out of the question. I wasn't going to have him walking around in my body without my being around to keep a careful eye on him.

Fair enough, I said, it's all yours.

I just relaxed, let everything go limp. My body didn't even sag. There was one weird and frightening moment when I watched my hands reach out for the switches, knowing that it wasn't me who was moving them. But the moment passed. I relaxed, utterly and completely. I sat back to watch. I already knew, after my experiences on Chao Phrya, the difficulties of being an absolutely passive observer. When you've been sovereign in your body for as long as I have, you get used to doing all sorts of things almost automatically—I don't mean reflex actions, because the reflexes would be just the same whichever one of us was in control—I mean things like thinking about Eve and glancing sideways to see what she was doing. Thought and action are much more closely related than we tend to think. While you're doing absolutely nothing but lying still and thinking—effectively what I was doing—your current of thought is producing all kinds of tiny actions to complement and corroborate your thoughts. Conscious application of senses, small changes of facial expression, just changes in bodily tension—all these are the products of consciousness. I could get away with it to a certain extent, but it takes only a very small conflict of nervous impulses to wreak havoc with coordination.

It was easier, this time, simply because I'd been through it before—in theory. I wasn't as worried or as fearful as I had been in the purple forest. But then, on that occasion the total demand on my body had been to stay perfectly still. The chance of conflict had been quite minimal. The present situation wasn't like that—now, I had to pretend to be perfectly immobile, absolutely impotent, while the wind trundled my body around in a perfect imitation of Grainger going about the business of keeping himself in one piece. *That* was difficult.

In the earlier months of our association—our symbiosis, as we would have it—it would have been impossible. My animosity toward him, my fear and my resentment of him, would have rendered me quite incapable of giving him my body to use as he wished. The conflict would have been inevitable. To do as I was doing needed perfect trust. Not perfect harmony—we never had that and never could have had it—but perfect *understanding*. A willingness to let him get on with it in his own way. A willingness not to be afraid of what might happen to my most precious possession through his carelessness or willful neglect. That asks a great deal of any man—maybe more of me than of most men, by virtue of my individualistic philosophy of life. A man just cannot be asked to do something like that without finding himself changed by the experience. That had been my initial fear of the wind—that my old identity would be eroded, forced to change. And it was justified. Grainger now was not Grainger as he had been when the *Javelin* went down on the rock that became Lapthorn's Grave. Grainger plus wind was a different being, unequal to the sum of the parts. I hadn't wanted him, and the reasons I hadn't wanted him and proved to be only too good. And yet here I was, playing possum in my own mind, letting the invader who'd changed me change me even more, *giving* him my body to use. It was necessary, absolutely necessary, for the demands of the present situation to be met, but that necessity in no way altered what was actually happening, the constraints it put upon me, the demands I had to meet. The fact remains that however necessary it was, I couldn't have done what I did without the existence of a very special relationship with the wind.

I call it perfect trust. Some might call it love.

I heard the clicks coming out of the call circuit—the clicks that meant we have contacted the *Cicindel*. I didn't know how long we had left, and I had no way of knowing what sort of message the wind was going to try to get across in whatever imitation Gallacellan he could make my voice produce. How long an explanation would the pilot of the *Cicindel* demand? How long an explanation could the wind produce?

I heard my voice begin to click. I can imagine no more eerie feeling than listening to your own voice conducting a conversation in a language you not only don't know, but aren't physically equipped for talking.

I had no real sense of passing time—measuring time is something which involves the accumulation of events, and the conscious involvement with said accumulation of events. Suspended in my functional limbo I felt quite out of touch with time. I could hear the clicking going on, but I had real difficulty in deciding which clicks came out of the call circuit and which out of me. I didn't feel involved with either set.

I knew that I could talk to the wind, and he could talk to me, but I didn't know when it was safe to do so. He never interrupted me when I was talking—and very rarely when I was listening to someone else talking. He was an adept at interposing his comments and questions into the blank spaces of life—the seconds in which nothing is happening, between events. Of course he was an adept—it was his way of life. But I was a stranger here. I didn't know how to pick my moments. So I waited, simply not knowing what was happening. I could see the screens—the wind was watching them intensely—but I didn't know what each showed. It should have been possible to work it out—visual representation ought to be the same in the two races, as we saw by the same wavelengths of light. But I didn't even occupy myself with that—my sensation of detachment was too great for me to explore the limited avenues by which I might involve my mind in events. I simply watched and waited, content to be a passenger in the whole affair.

In a sense, the rest was a great relief to me. I had been on the move and under pressure for a long time now. The hours I'd spent in my bunk on the *Swan* between the dive and the drive had been recuperation, not rest. This enforced relaxation was the first in a long time. To some extent, I needed it.

Keep smiling, the wind's silent voice said to me, we're winning. The *Cicindel* is safe. Alone we did it.

—Can I have my body back now? I asked.

I know you're not going to like this, he said, but I don't think that's wise. Of course, if you cut up rough, I'll have to let you have it, but if you want my sincere advice you'll stay exactly where you are and let me handle this.

—Screw your sincere advice, I said. You always sincerely reckoned you'd be a better me than I am. I want my body back, and you better give me reasons why I shouldn't have it.

We're still in trouble, remember? This ship is heading for God knows where under its own steam, following a program we know nothing about and carrying a cloud of absolute destruction a million miles across. Now, that isn't funny, and we have to find a way of switching this thing off. I've read these labels and I've looked at these tapes, and I just *don't know*. We need help to sort this out and there's only one place where the help we need is available right now. That's the *Cicindel*. I don't know how much they know about this ship, but they knew enough to send out a warning, even if they did send it to the wrong places. I can talk to them.

—What about Stylaster? I demanded. He surely knows more than anyone else.

Stylaster is going to want to know who I am, he pointed out. What do I tell him?

—The truth.

You know I can't do that. If *any* of this bunch find out it's a human that's clicking at them they're apt to slap up their wall of silence. The guy I've got now knows something is wrong, but at least he thinks I'm a Gallacellan. On this basis, we can deal. Who knows what might happen if the truth gets out? Let me play it, Grainger, please. You must see that it's our best chance. Maybe our only chance. If we don't find out how to control this ship we have no chance whatsoever of getting back down to Johnny and the captain.

—All right, I said—reluctantly, but what choice had I? It's your baby. But just do me one favor. There's no point in us playing musical chairs, so I'll stay put. But contact Nick and Johnny. Let's at least find out whether they're alive. And tell them to stay put.

I can't, he said.

—What do you mean *can't*?

The caller, he said, it's jammed. Maslax broke a switch. I can call the *Cicindel*, but that's all. I can't call the Gallacellans on Iniomi. I can't call the *Swan* or Pallant or the human base on Iniomi.

—All right, I said. All right. Just go ahead. Don't mind me. I'll just sit here and watch. Just get us out of this mess.

My body turned around, and I found myself looking at Eve. She stood beside Maslax, who was crumpled up like a rag doll, having lost interest in the whole affair. She had the gun in one hand and the small remote-control bomb-trigger in the other. She had an air of astonished patience. She had just been watching me do the impossible.

"It's OK," I heard my voice say. "We're safe, for now. We have time in hand to sort things out."

She just went on staring, for a moment. It seemed oddly incredible to me that she didn't automatically notice that it was someone else using my voice and not me. But how could she possibly suspect?

"Nobody speaks Gallacellan," she said.

"That's right," I heard myself say, "nobody speaks Gallacellan. Once we're out of this, you can wonder how we got out for the rest of your life. For now, let's just go on doing the impossible quietly, hey?"

It was a perfect imitation. I had to admit that. My voice, my dryness, my slightly aggressive manner. All just perfect. He was more like me than I am—on an off-day.

My eyes swung back to the instrument panel, and began to scan.

I clicked furiously. The call circuit clicked back. I knew we were in for a very long session, but I was damned if I was going to sleep. Instead, I reflected on one or two of the wrong conclusions I'd jumped to. There was one hell of a lot packed into a short space of time. Ordinarily, I am a top-class conclusion-jumper, and very accurate. But to err is human, and everybody's talent lets him down sometimes.

It was all a matter of misunderstanding. The Gallacellan/human wall of silence. The failure to communicate. I knew a bit better now. I could even see why I had been wrong about the Fenris device. The *Varsovien* was an emigration ship—that much was obvious. Not a warship at all. I had concluded that she would not be armed because I had been thinking of her simply as "Gallacellan." It hadn't occurred to me that there was an enemy to arm her against. A simple enough flaw in reasoning. But this ship dated from the Gallacellan wars, when there were Gallacellans and Gallacellans. This magnificent ship wasn't the pride and joy of the entire race—it was the ultimate escape route planned and constructed by one side in the war. It hadn't been used. Either that particular side won, or peace came and the Gallacellans decided to patch up their civilization together. Of course the *Varsovien* was armed. With the ultimate weapon—the ultimate *defensive* weapon. The people on the ship couldn't fire it in anger—it was a faculty built into the reactive mechanism of the ship. The *Varsovien* was a gigantic cocoon—a generation ship which could look after itself and house a million people—maybe more. If left alone, it would simply have transferred and gone. If attacked, well, it would stick around for a while and let the attackers come. Then, after they'd had their fill, transcee and off we go. Typically Gallacellan, now I came to think about it. A prey species' ultimate dream. Perfect armor. The predators could do all they wanted—to no avail. The perfect passive resistance. *Honi soit qui mal y pense.*

That left just two questions: Why did Stylaster's Gallacellans want the *Varsovien* back? And why did the *Cicindel* contingent want to stop them? But those were questions of purely academic interest. A third question—a much more urgent and important question—dawned on me while I dwelt idly on the first two.

Prey mentality. Perfect armor. The ultimate defense. The *Varsovien* would have no switch for turning the Fenris device on. Would it have one for turning it off?

12

There's one way, said the wind. Just one way.

—It's just not one, I told him. There has to be an easy way. Damn it, this thing's nothing more than a machine. It works with circuits and wires and networks and synapses just like any other machine. All we have to do is break one wire, one synapse. All we need is just one wrench in the right part of the works. Your way is just pure madness.

Look, said the wind, without as much patience as I might have shown if the relative positions were reversed— that is to say, normal—this is a big ship. This is a very, very big ship. It may be a machine, but it is a machine on a scale you have never, ever, envisaged in all your life. Yes, it needs only one pair of wire cutters or one wrench. But we just don't have access to the right wire or the right works. The guys on the *Cicindel* are good, but hell, they're a million miles away from a ship they've never seen, talking to a linguistic incompetent. Sure, if we had three weeks or a month, sure we could get enough information to them. They could work things out. They could talk us through it. We could find the tools and the plans and we could do the work with pinpoint accuracy. But, Grainger, this ship is accelerating. In fifty minutes or less it is going to make tachyonic transfer and cut us off from the *Cicindel*. Maybe forever. Do you want to go to Andromeda? Do you want to take a million-mile bomb to Andromeda?

—But what are you suggesting, I said, still bewildered, is *blowing up the ship*.

I'm proposing to do just what you want, said the wind. Cut the circuit. Stop the machine. Turn the Fenris device off and keep the *Varsovien* in normal space. As far as the people on the *Cicindel*—and as far as I myself—can see there is just one way to be sure of doing that in the time available and that is to burn out the brain that's coordinating the machine. They can tell me exactly how to do that from right here, and they can tell me exactly how much time we have in hand to get out of this room, off of this deck, and deep enough into the bowels of the ship so that we aren't burned out with it. Now is that or isn't it the *only* thing we can do?

—What about Johnny? I said. What about the captain? Who's going to bring *them* back, if we only have standard ships? Are you going to go down in the *Cicindel* and get them out? Are you?

That, of course, was a silly question.

If necessary, he said, that's exactly what I'll do. What good are we going to be to Johnny and Nick if we're in a flying coffin on our way out of the galaxy? We have to take our problems one at a time, and the one we have at this time is: How do we get out of here? And there's only one way we know. Just one. Burn the brain and run like hell. As soon as the defense mechanism cuts out the *Cicindel* will come in and pick us up. They'll know exactly where we'll be. *Then* we can worry about another drop to Mormyr. Maybe Nick can bring the ship up. Maybe we can get the *Sister Swan* operational in time. Maybe the Gallacellans have a ship we can at least *try* it in. But first, we've got to be free to try it. We have to save ourselves first. You're arguing with the inevitable.

And I was, of course. There was no way of turning the Fenris device off—not just like *that*. In the time we had available, there was only one method—outright brutality. We had to cripple the whole damn ship. I had my suspicions about the helpful people aboard the *Cicindel*—they hadn't wanted the ship lifted, maybe they had a vested interest in her being destroyed. Maybe they were holding out on us. Maybe there *was* an easy way, apart from just cutting loose and blasting. But how could we know? We were in their hands. At their mercy. They were calling the odds. We had no alternative but to do as they told us, and wait in some cubbyhole a mile or two downstairs for them to come in and pick us up. And suppose it didn't work? Suppose the Fenris device *didn't* cut out? For our next trick . . .

But it was pointless worrying about that. It was pointless worrying at all. We had to do what we had to do.

I felt my body begin to get back into my suit, and I heard my voice tell Eve to do the same. Then I heard me tell Maslax that he could either come with us under his own steam or not at all, because Eve and I would have enough to do carrying Ecdyon. Dragging Ecdyon, more like.

Maslax made no reply, and the wind wasn't wasting any time waiting for him to show some signs of interest. My body was already back at the console, clicking away into the speaker.

We turned away abruptly.

"Right," said my voice. "Let's get Ecdyon into the prerambulating cubicle."

Eve and my body took an arm each, and began to heave. I supposed that if the wind was finished clicking now I could ask to take over again, but I knew he wouldn't see it that way. This was his show—it was a maneuver he'd initiated—he had some right to see it through. I had to concede him that, like it or not.

We managed to bundle Ecdyon through the door into the smaller chamber. He stirred, and made some awkward noises that might have been the Gallacellan equivalent of cries of pain, but he didn't show any signs of being aware of what was going on, despite the fact that all four of his eyes were still open.

I felt my body hesitate for just a moment, then I found

myself kneeling over Maslax, doing up his suit. I didn't
bother fastening his helmet—just hauled him up by the
scruff of the neck, threw him into the elevator with Eve
and the Gallacellan, and then threw the helmet in after
him.

"Throw me the gun," said my voice, to Eve.

She complied, and the wind let go a few last clicks at
the caller. Then we backed up into the doorway, he took
careful aim, adjusted the beam, and launched a needlelike
ray into the wall just below the console.

Then there was more waiting, while the needle ate its
way through the wall, and the chamber filled with smoke.
An alarm bell went off close at hand, and we jumped
spasmodically. But the wind lost the aim for only a fraction of a second. Then white fire began gouting out of the
hole in the wall, and electric sparks, and a series of sharp,
crackly explosions. I felt my left hand grip the door and
my body poise itself to jump. I felt my eyes get hot, and
vision was lost in a dazzling glare.

Then we leaped backward, slammed the door, slammed
the door of the elevator, and punched a button. We didn't
need to pause to wonder which button. The wind was really on his toes.

For one terrible moment I thought we weren't going to
move, and then I felt the gentle tug of sidewise acceler-
ation as we began our retreat, amid the ever-increasing
clamor of alarm bells. I was listening for a big bang, not
knowing whether to hope or expect to hear it immediately
or when we were well away from the hot spot. Without
my sense of time, the waiting was horribly distorted. We
seemed to be stuck inside a single moment, moving inside
a tiny, featureless cylinder, while all around us a machine
as big as a world went mad. If the *Gray Goose* had been
an ant attacking a whale, then what were we, inside the
whale? Not Jonah, for sure. Bacteria, maybe. Perhaps not
even that. Allergens setting off a vast chain reaction affect-
ing the whole body. Tiny molecules sending the *Varsovien* into anaphylactic shock.

We transferred from the horizontal conveyor to the ver-

tical. Again, we took Ecdyon through first, and again we
had to go back to carry Maslax. He was absolutely
inert—not dead, not even unconscious. Completely coma-
tose.

Down we went.

I knew it would be much farther down than across, that
the descent would take far longer. But I still couldn't feel
the waiting. I was still isolated from the sequence of
events, suspended like a fly in amber in a little shell of
nothing that owned neither time nor space. I was nowhere.
And yet I existed. I was a part of it all, if not a participant. I was there.

My body kicked Maslax a few times—quite without
malice—trying to remind him that life was still going on.
Eve was busy looking at Ecdyon, trying to find signs of
life.

The alarm bells went on and on, as if the whole ship
was filled with nothing but alarm bells, and still the big
bang had not happened. Still we were dropping. I was
conscious of movements—my own and Eve's, but I was
taking little notice. The movements seemed meaningless.
A few words floated past, but I didn't hear them. I had
determined previously that I was going to listen and
remember every single word that the wind used my voice
to say, but that seemed unimportant now.

Then we stopped again, and I felt my arm reach out to
grip the door handle. I felt my brain register something
that made my hand hesitate. The handle which had begun
to turn stopped, and my grip on it became suddenly in-
tense. I tried to regain a temporal integration with events,
just some connection, so that I would know what was
happening, and what was wrong.

I heard my voice say: "There's no air out there."

It made no immediate impact. I was suited. I had my
helmet on. I was breathing my own air, from my own
backpack. What did it matter what was in the corridor or
the other chamber?

Then I remembered Ecdyon. His suit was holed.

I needed all of that timeless instant then. Time stopped

dead while I isolated myself from it and tried to see. I could feel the tightness of my hand's grip against the door—a grip the wind would not relax. I knew that the decision he was making would take less than a second. He had no more time. We had to get to a place of safety before the bang and the cut-out of the ship's functions. We had to get into an airlock, from which the *Cicindel* could rescue us. If the power cut out and the lift fell . . . they'd never find us. We'd be dead.

I could almost feel the thoughts jumbled into that split second—almost pick them up one by one and read them. Ecdyon: seven feet tall. No other suit. No patch. Ecdyon: dead.

My hand turned the handle, and opened the lock.

"Open the other door!" my voice howled at Eve.

My body dived to Ecdyon's side, took a firm hold, and even while Eve was still opening the door we were pulling him through. Eve went back for Maslax. She'd already put his helmet back on during the descent. He was all right.

I think, if she hadn't gone back, the wind would have left him. I think the wind would have opted to save those extra few seconds by shutting the airlock door as quickly as possible and flooding the place with air from the pressure-system just that fraction sooner. But Eve went back, seconds wasted while she was clumsily pushing him through the lock. She had neither the strength nor the speed for a smooth operation. But we got him through, we got the door shut, and we threw the air-valve open.

And nothing happened. The tank was empty. One of the missiles from the *Gray Goose* had cracked the supply system, and the air had gone out through the outer skin. Including the air from the lock.

Ecdyon died there, on the floor of the chamber.

13

People do die. It's one of the facts of—ha ha—life. A lot of people died in the Halcyon Drift, including Alachakh, who was my friend. A couple of guys got plugged on Rhapsody, for no very good reason. Men died on Pharos. If the chances had turned out a little different on Chao Phrya, people could have been killed there, too. Ferrier was dead, and his girl. The crew of the *Gray Goose* was dead.

By all this, I remained relatively unaffected.

But to have a man die deside me—to have him die as a direct consequence of my own actions—that was different. In a way, I was even responsible for the fact that his suit was holed in the first place. If I'd chosen to warn Maslax about the orientation of the artificial gravity field, the gun need never have gone off.

I still held that gun. I still had it in my hand. Throughout the entire sequence—opening doors, pulling bodies about, pressing buttons—I had never let go of that gun, as if my life depended on my hand sticking to it, never letting it go.

So maybe it *was* the wind. What difference did that make?

None at all.

I don't like people dying. I don't even like people getting hurt. If it happens close at hand, it makes me sick. I felt a little sick then. Nothing comparable had happened to me since the *Javelin* went down, since I failed to save the ship, since I failed to flip the ship, and since the crash had killed Michael Lapthorn, who was also—I guess—my friend.

I had already had enough. I had already decided to quit and get out and go somewhere where the action was stone cold and people weren't dropping dead or hanging worlds in the balance on all sides of me. This came on top of my having had enough. It was adding injury to insult.

The purring in the walls of the ship was dying slowly and progressively. There was no big bang, no convulsions, no screaming. The *Varsovien* died as quietly as had Ecdyon. Discreetly.

The light in the airlock was out. I had a light mounted on my backpack, along with a spare air-bottle, but I didn't bother to switch it on. We waited in the pitch-darkness, saying nothing except for the occasional remark about how much time it might take, or was taking.

I had taken command back from the wind. We weren't reckoning on needing any more Gallacellan. Everyone except Eve would take it for granted that it was Ecdyon who had done all the talking. He wouldn't be arguing the point. I reckoned that if I never said another word about it, Eve would never be sure enough of herself to start talking. That had worked before. She still didn't know what had happened aboard the *Lost Star*. All attempts to find out had simply been met with stony silence. She had dropped the matter eventually—what else could she do?

It was a long wait. I almost wished that I'd left the wind in the hot seat, so that I wouldn't have had to feel the passing of time minute by minute—I could have felt it all at once. But that would have been a sort of suicide, a preference for nonexistence. Unlike the wind, I am exclusively a creature of body-and-soul. I don't have his versatility. Backseat driving was his way of life, but to me it was more a way of death. One can't just opt out of bad and boring moments of life. That's futile. So I did my own waiting, and my own worrying, and I lived within my own misery.

Eventually, we heard them. My helmet was resting against the metal casing of the lock, and I heard them outside the lock. They weren't opening the lock—they didn't do that for quite some time. At first, I couldn't figure out what they *were* doing, but eventually I realized they were connecting the locks. They were running a corridor from their ship to this one. I wondered if they knew whether the lock was cracked and that if they tried to flood it with air they'd have to patch it up pretty smartly. It didn't matter much—they'd have it to spare.

It wasn't until they actually began to open the door that I realized what their lights were going to show them.

One dead Gallacellan, with a gunshot wound in his chest. One Grainger, still holding the gun. I couldn't even drop the damn thing, because we were in free fall owing to the ship's switching off. It would just float around the lock with us, like a big ugly wasp.

The lock swung open, and the Gallacellans came in. There were two of them—suited. About ten meters of white corridor was behind them, and then another lock, outer door open, inner closed.

We had to take turns going through the *Cicindel's* lock—two at a time. Eve and I went first. I didn't look either of our rescuers in the face. I just couldn't. I stuck the gun out of sight, in the pack, but my hand still felt hot, as if it were carrying the mark of Cain, or something.

Beyond the lock there was light aplenty, gravity (a fraction more than E-normal), and air (the same sharp air that we breathed aboard the *Varsovien*). There were also Gallacellans. Two more of them. Waiting for us. I took my helmet off, and this time I couldn't help looking at them.

I couldn't tell by looking what caste they might be.

"Anybody speak English?" I asked. There was no answer.

Eve and I stood to one side to let the lock open and close again. One of the Gallacellans came through, carrying Maslax as if the little man were just a rag doll. The alien deposited his burden on the floor, conveniently to one side. I didn't bother to go to him, and neither did Eve. Just at that moment, we didn't particularly care what was going to happen to Maslax in the near future or at any other time up to and including the day of judgment. We had had enough of Maslax.

We waited, until the last Gallacellan came back, carrying Ecdyon.

I wished that Gallacellans changed expression, so that I could know what one or more of them might be thinking. But they stood there as if they were movie props made out of rubber.

"We tried," I said, pointlessly. "We really did try."

Ominous silence. They looked at me, and I felt accused, even though there was nothing in their faces but the usual blank features.

One of them turned his back on me and clicked.

What did he say? I asked the wind.

—He wants to know how come you speak Gallacellan," he said.

And I laughed. I don't really know what I'd been expecting. Accusations, questions, just sarcastic comments. I don't know. But not this.

"I don't," I said, in English, then realized that it was a silly thing to say, and corrected it to: "I don't understand." I spread my hands wide and tried to look ingenuous.

—It's no good, said the wind. I think he knows.

How?

—I really did try, he said. I tried, but there just wasn't any way. I just didn't sound like a Gallacellan. I got all the caste-forms right, I'm sure about that. But you haven't got the voice for it. They must have figured us out right away. Even over the circuit.

One Gallacellan sounds pretty much like another to me, but I had to admit that they handled their language a lot better than the wind had. He was right. I wasn't built for it.

OK, I said tiredly. You'd better tell them what happened. But keep in touch, hey? Just once now and again, if you have a moment, give me a quick summary.

It was so easy just to pass back inside my own skull. I surprised myself. My body didn't even stagger. A perfectly smooth operation. I knew I was getting used to it and I didn't like it. But playing a completely passive role is like riding a bicycle—you don't forget how to do it. The level of control remains the same—one slip and your body is in trouble—and it never becomes *easy*. But you get used to it. You acquire the touch. I didn't particularly want to acquire the touch. Privately, I swore that it would never happen again—that I would never get into a situation where I *needed* it to happen again. I promised myself, faithfully.

After the clicking had gone on for a few moments, I asked the wind whether the Gallacellan believed us. It seemed to me likely that he wouldn't. It was a long and complicated and fairly incredible story.

I don't think he even cares, the wind told me. He doesn't give a damn about Ecdyon—he's too high caste for that. He hasn't even bothered to ask who shot him, let alone why. He doesn't want to know what we were doing on the *Varsovien*, or why. He just wants to know who taught us Gallacellan.

—What've you told him?" I asked.

I'm telling him, he assured me. Worry not, I'm telling him.

—The truth?

You have to be joking. He wouldn't believe it. I've told him we learned it by listening, by studying, by watching. I've told him that the Library has put together all that the human race knows about Gallacellans, and that we've found out quite a lot. I'm going to talk to him some more, about mutual understanding and the benefits of communication.

—Who the hell do you think you are? I said. Titus Charlot?

But I got no answer. He was clicking again.

We didn't have to stand in the corridor long. They took

us into a cabin—a big cabin, fitted out so finely and neatly
that it just *had* to be the captain's cabin. They only wanted
me—or, to be strictly accurate, they only wanted the wind.
But Eve was nervous, and she wanted to stick with me.
They didn't object. Maslax they took somewhere else. I
never saw him again. I believe that his interest in the world
revived after a period of time in Iniomi, but they never
gave him back his job in the Library, nor even sent him
back to Pallant. I think he ended up on Airn, the second
world of the system, but whether he was in jail, in the hos-
pital, or what the hell I simply do not know. I never
wanted to know enough to find out.

The wind talked to the captain for several hours while
the *Cicindel* flew to Iniomi. Occasionally, he slid back
some small packet of information about what he was
trying to do, or what the captain was telling him. But I
never got a full transcript of the conversation and I guess
I never will.

The wind wanted to be the human race's first diplomatic
mission to the Gallacellans. He wanted to do Charlot's
work for him and set up a basis for negotiation. He had
big plans, did the wind. But he always was an optimist.

He hadn't got a cat in hell's chance. I guessed that
pretty soon, and I think he probably knew it all along, but
wanted to try anyway.

The Gallacellan wall of indifference hasn't come into
being simply because they don't like humans. Basically,
the Gallacellans are an indifferent people. They've culti-
vated it in their civilization, and no doubt it was there for
them to cultivate. A defensive mentality. They owned to
no priorities except survival, and their chief priority was
ensuring that survival—ensuring it against all possible
eventualities. Fair enough. That's the name of the game.
That's evolution for you. He who survives is the fittest, by
definition. Man is an evolutionary gold-medal winner because he is an *active* survivor. Some people might claim
that he has a basically nasty mind. He is an omnivorous
grabber—a possessor. But that's not the only kind of fit-
ness that wins out in the good old struggle for existence.

The Gallacellans were gold-medal survivors as well, only the Gallacellan is a *passive* survivor.

He is always around to fight another day (but never today.) He runs away. When caught, he is difficult to kill, but basically he is difficult to catch. The Gallacellan would far rather live in peace than not. He likes to know where he stands. He likes to know he is safe. The Gallacellan society is carefully structured, and so is the language, to allow maximum communication where it is needed, and none at all where it is not. The caste system is absolute. The notion of privacy is central to the Gallacellan civilization. That such a civilization is imperfect is manifestly obvious. But it is just as manifestly obvious that the human civilization is totally unstable, and just as imperfect, and contains just as many contradictions. That it works is also manifestly obvious.

There is, as they say, more than one way to skin a cat.

But when all the analyzing and philosophizing is done, there remains one simple fact. The Gallacellans are not interested in talking to one another, save for definite social purposes. They do not indulge in merry chitchat. All their communication is functional, helping to keep the race in good condition and surviving as well as possible. There is no conceivable reason why they should want to become interested in talking to humans, except insofar as it is strictly functional. And the Gallacellans have a caste to decide what is and is not strictly functional.

They are narrow-minded. So are we. The overlap is very slight indeed.

The wind argued for a long time. I know that he argued hard, and I believe that he argued well. But he could not break caste. Whatever he said that was outside what the captain wanted to hear the captain simply would not and did not hear. Despite the fact that they were speaking the same language, they failed to communicate. Except insofar as it was strictly functional—as the captain defined function.

The wind made not the slightest dent in the wall of indifference. The situation remained the same. It had a certain deadly irony. The only Gallacellans with whom we could really communicate were the ones who could speak human languages. That was because it was their designated function to communicate. But *their* communication with other Gallacellans was strictly limited, defined by other functions. They couldn't use their understanding any more than I could use mine. Titus Charlot, not for the first time, was simply going to have to reconcile himself to the fact that he wasn't going to unite the contents of the human and the Gallacellan minds inside one of his analogue machines. It was just not on.

—If they knew you weren't a Gallacellan all along, I said, why did they rescue us?

In the interests of peaceful coexistence, the wind told me. And because they needed to know how come I could make myself understood.

So none of us got what we wanted. We set down on Iniomi without being able to tell the captain how we knew his language, but without convincing him it was a good idea to promote interracial relations. Out of the hours of talk came precisely nothing.

But we did get home safe. Well, perhaps not home exactly, but back to *terra firma*. Back to Titus Charlot.

14

"Get me a ship," I said.

He looked tired. I didn't see why it should have put years on *him*. Years on *me,* sure. But not years on him. He'd done nothing but sit and wait.

"Are you going to tell me about it?" he inquired.

"Not now," I said. "I want a ship. A good ship, with a good pilot and a good engineer. I don't care where you find them, but get them fast. I want to talk to the *Hooded Swan.*

We were in the boss's office, on Iniomi. The boss was there, but he was just so much decoration. Charlot was running things in Iniomi and had been for some time. Stylaster wasn't there. I wasn't particularly interested in where he'd gone. I could catch up on the news about Stylaster while Charlot was catching up on the news about the *Varsovien.* All in good time.

They had a circuit rigged up right there in the office. Charlot just waved me to it.

I beeped the *Swan.*

"Captain delArco speaking," came back the answer. Right away. He was on hand, waiting for me. He must have been waiting for me for some time.

"It's Grainger," I said.

"Are you OK?" he asked.

"Just great," I said. "But you're in a mess. You know what goes on?"

"You lifted the other ship," he said. "After that, it gets confused. But you're up there and we're down here, right?"

"That's it," I said.

"But we aren't blown to bits," he added. "Just lucky, I guess."

"Sure," said, "we're on a real lucky streak."

"Are you going to tell me how to lift this thing?" he asked. His voice was taut. That wasn't what he wanted. He was scared. He wanted me to be a hero and go down to get him. But he was too much of a gentleman ever to say so. And besides—he didn't figure me for a hero.

Neither did I, much.

"You wouldn't stand a chance," I told him.

"So what do we do?" he said.

"That depends," I said coolly. "It depends on your friend and employer Titus Charlot."

There was a silence. Neither Nick nor Charlot knew whose prerogative it was to ask me what the hell I meant. Perhaps they knew—Charlot, anyhow.

I filled the silence myself.

"This is the way it is," I said. "The only ship good enough to go down is already down, and the only pilot good enough to bring it up is already up. Now we have two choices. You can risk your life, and Johnny's life, and the ship, trying to lift. Or I can risk my life trying to drop. Now that might look like two to one your way, but it's really three to two. If you try, and fail, you both die. If I try, and fail, we all three die. That's the way it is."

"Nobody's quarreling," said Nick. His voice was very dry.

"The difference is," I said, "that I think I can do it and I know you can't. So I think maybe I ought to come get you. The only question I ask myself is—is it worth it? See? Now you know that I'm a real son of a bitch. But you also know that I owe you a favor or two, and that Johnny's grandfather was a very good friend of mine. I'll bring you back for free, and I'll bring Johnny back for free. But for the *Hooded Swan,* I want a salvage fee. You know why and you know how much. You see my point, Nick, don't you?"

"I know," said Nick.

I turned to Charlot. "You do see what I mean, now, don't you? You own me. You have a two-year lease on my soul. Because of a salvage fee. Because of a nasty little joke that Caradoc played on me after they rescued me by mistake. You bought that joke, Titus. You paid twenty thousand for a lousy joke. Well I *never* laughed, and I'm not laughing now. I quit, Titus, and that's final. Absolute. You can send me right to jail, right now. You can have me put away for so long that I'll be finished—never fly another ship. But your ship is down on Mormyr, Titus, and it has half its crew aboard. So the joke's on you, isn't it? How do *you* feel?"

"You wouldn't leave them down there," said Charlot. "You'd go down to get them no matter what I say. I know you, Grainger."

"You know I'm no hero."

"I know you're no hero. But that isn't what's important. You're a hard-minded man, Grainger. You don't bend. You place yourself outside it all. If you were a hero, I wouldn't have had to buy you in the first place. If you'd have been a hero, you wouldn't have been rotting on that rock so that one day you could be bought. You're an isolated man. Untouched by human hand. You live inside yourself. Nothing else matters but you. And your mind's already made up. You know you can bring them back. And you're going to do it. For your own reasons. For your own self-importance. For your own tiny omnipotence. So you can continue to place yourself outside it all. So you can leave it alone with a clean sheet. Because if you left them there, you'd be *involved.*"

"I want twenty thousand salvage fee for bringing up the *Swan,*" I said. "Do I get it?"

"You're a member of her crew," he said. "You can't claim it."

"I already quit," I said. "And whether I can claim it or not doesn't figure. You can give it to me out of the goodness of your heart."

"All right," he said simply. "If that's what you want. Bring back the *Swan* and you're free. I'll get a draft covering every hour you put in on your contract. Every penny. It won't be enough to buy a ship."

"Never mind that," I said. "What about a ship to take me down?"

"I thought you said it couldn't be done," he said.

"I don't intend to land. That's why I want a pilot. I just want him to do a curve. Just a long arc. In and out. No maneuvering, no hovering, no landing. He can take me as low as he dares and then I'll jump."

I could tell by his open mouth that the boss was impressed. Not so Charlot. He already knew what I intended. It was obvious. There's never any problem about getting down. Things *fall* down. The problem is getting down in a fit condition to come up again. If a ship could take me to the clouds, I could ride out the storm in a small life-raft. Sure it would crash. Sure I could get hurt. But just so long as I hit that expanse of rock close enough to the *Swan* I should be in a condition fit enough to reach her and fly her out. There were a lot of things that could go wrong, and a guy could get killed trying tricks like that. But it could work. And it was the only way.

"There's a ship coming out from Pallant," said Titus. "The best they have. I can get better from New Alexandria, but it would take time."

"We'll use what we have," I said. "The ship's anchored down there, but in that sort of weather she's taking one hell of a pounding. I want her as fit as possible for a lift. Have you got a pilot?"

"A good one."

"A liner jockey?"

"An independent. He isn't a hero either. We bought him too."

"And the engineer?"

"The whole outfit. As a package."

"How much did you offer *them?*"

Charlot smiled. "Fifty," he said.

"Fifty?"

"Thousand," he added. "If they succeed, that is. They don't get anything if it doesn't work. It's a salvage fee."

"So OK," I said. "You got me cheap. Lucky you."

"You didn't have to go through all that," he told me.

"Like hell," I said. "Are you trying to tell me that if I'd come here, said how do you do, and then gone down to get the ship, then you'd have fallen all over me and said 'Here's your money, good-bye and good luck'?"

"I'm not talking about the deal," he said. "I'm talking about the performance. I'm talking about the way you opened that circuit, and still have it open, so that you could shout out loud to everyone concerned that you weren't doing it for nothing, that you were only doing it for the money. It wasn't necessary. It's futile. You're a fool, Grainger."

"Yeah," I said, "maybe I am. I'm signing off here, Nick. I need some rest before this ship arrives. I'll be with you when I can."

I closed the circuit, without giving him a chance to say anything. I didn't want to listen.

I walked out of the room. The man who ran things on Iniomi just didn't understand. He looked totally bemused. Titus watched me go. I don't think he understood either, though he thought he did. I wasn't even sure that I understood.

—OK, said the wind. You're out. Out of it all. Not just the job, but the whole thing. You're going to pick them up, and you've done your level best to make them hate you for doing it. But do you really think it'll work? Do you really think that they'll believe the act? I think they'll thank you for it anyway. I think they'll love you for it.

They don't have to, I told him. It's just something I have to do. It's not for them. Not for them at all. It's my show. There's no one I'd take risks for except myself.

—You're running away, said the wind. Ever since I got into your mind on that black mountain, you've been running away. All you want to do is find yourself a hole and hide. You're stacking excuses a mile high. You don't like Charlot, you don't like the political situation, you don't like being under an obligation. Even your fear and the fact that you don't like violence are just excuses. You're running away because of sheer habit. It's a way of life. You've got a Gallacellan mentality, Grainger.

The Gallacellans do all right, I told him. They survive.

—It's not enough, he told me. Even they know that.

And it seemed that they did. Some of them. The men from the *Cicindel* obviously thought survival wasn't enough. They had tried to stop Stylaster using the *Varsovien*.

But I wasn't so sure that my sympathies weren't with Stylaster. I'd worked out, by logic alone, why he wanted the ship so badly. There was no way of confirming the guess, but I was pretty sure. I'd been right when I said the *Varsovien* was an emigration ship. It was the ultimate escape device—the ultimate insurance. It could take a million Gallacellans right out of the galaxy, and it had a Fenris device to see that *nothing*—absolutely nothing—could stop them.

The Gallacellan wars had ended without the *Varsovien* being needed. It was needed again now. But not because the Gallacellans saw another breakup in their civilization. They were afraid of something else entirely.

They were afraid of us. The human race.

And who could blame them? The expansion of the companies was *devouring* the galaxy. The balance between the companies and New Rome plus New Alexandria was delicate enough to explode at a touch. War was coming. War between the companies and the law, war between the companies and each other. War between human and alien. Titus Charlot and a couple of thousand like him thought they could keep the lid on. Maybe they could. For ten years, a hundred, a thousand. But not forever. Who could blame the Gallacellans for being scared? Hell, *I* was scared. I wanted out. All the way out. I wanted a nice little niche where I could hide. A little corner which wasn't worth fighting about, where I could handle my ship my way without interference. That was what the Gallacellans wanted too, and Stylaster had been prepared to go to Andromeda to find it. But the Gallacellans had their differences of opinion too. The *Cicindel* had tried to tip us off—tried to make us leave the *Varsovien* where she lay. And they had brought it off. Somehow.

Maybe they wanted the ship for themselves. More likely, though, they didn't approve of Stylaster's methods. I think they didn't want us to find out that the ship was an escape ship. I think they wanted us to think it was a warship. They didn't want us to know how scared they were. Because they knew as little about us as we knew about them, and they could understand just as little of what they did know.

They purely and simply didn't want to reveal themselves.

Prey mentality.

Maybe the wind was right. Maybe I do have a mind like a Gallacellan.

15

There was a long wait. Once the ship had come out from Pallant we had all the downship men on Iniomi poking about in her guts. She needed a complete checkout, and then she had to be fitted out to do the job we needed her to do.

I let Charlot supervise the hardware. It was, I suppose, most unlike me to entrust a job like that to another man. In my "normal" state of mind I am extremely suspicious about hardware, and I like to supervise its organization right down to the last spring-catch. But my state of mind at this particular time was somewhat charged with tension, and a certain amount of resentment at the whole pattern of events. In addition, I was tired—not physically, but mentally tired, exhausted by heavy thought and the pace of happenings.

I had other things to do besides check the rig that was supposed to deliver me to the surface in one piece. Primarily, I had to talk to the man who was going to take me down. I had nothing in particular to say to him—there was no vital piece of information about conditions in the lower atmosphere that I could pass on to him, and I knew that if I tried to reorganize his flight-plan for him he'd get upset. I would have. But I needed to talk to him anyway, to find out for myself that he was capable of doing what was needed.

The ship was called the *Coregon,* and it was a compact but very solid mass-relaxation ship. She was very slow, by transport standards, but she was designed for work in atmosphere, and in dirty space. She carried far more power than she was able to use just for pushing herself along. Her one big failing was in her almost-total lack of maneuverability. Within her limitations she was a good ship, but once her limitations were reached, she became so much scrap-iron. Well, that was all right—I didn't intend that she should go anywhere she wasn't equipped to go.

Her captain, pilot, and owner was a man named Jacks. He told me only his surname and that was the only name I ever knew him by. That's a matter of etiquette—real spacemen don't have first names. Not many of them go as far as me and do without altogether, but while in space, operating independently, they abandon whatever other names they might have been born with, and only pick them up again when they're down for a good long spell.

I liked Jacks. He was nearly as old as me and he'd been in space even longer. He hadn't put in anything like the distances I'd clocked up, but he'd never had a partner like Lapthorn. He'd worked for his living, pretty solidly, doing more or less the same job, for all his life. He'd seen virtually nothing of the expanding rim.

He didn't like me. That was understandable. It was nothing personal—just the fact that the present job was very unpleasant, and just because he was going to do it didn't mean that he was going to like it as well. He was ready to talk to me because he was as keen to find out what kind of lunatic I was as I was to find out about him.

He told me that his ship was guaranteed against any damage and that he was still too young to die, but that the big money he had been offered—the offer he couldn't refuse—was dependent upon my pulling off the crazy stunt. He wanted to know what my chances were.

To be quite honest, I had no idea. It wasn't the kind of thing one could measure against precedent. It seemed fairly simple—I'd have a heavy-duty suit with a big power-pack (very uneconomical, but I was only going to use it once) which should see me through once I was on-surface. You can shoot bricks at a heavy-duty suit and they just bounce off, so the hailstones wouldn't bother me. They're virtually impossible to knock over, so the storm-winds wouldn't be any real problem. Even the biggest power-packs die the death after ten or twelve hours, because the demands of just lifting the suit are so heavy, but ten or twelve hours ought to give me time, just so long as we got our sums right. The life raft was one big problem—I couldn't just come down in a shell, because there was apt to be one hell of a bump when I hit the ground. There had to be an ejector and it had to be rigged to compensate for virtually all of the momentum I'd pick up while I was falling through the clouds. Life rafts with ejectors we had—rigging the ejector was something else again. Parachutes were out of the question in that mess, so I had to come down with some sort of bump. The problem of minimizing the bump so that it would leave both suit and Grainger in full working order was largely a problem in absolute timing. That was Charlot's problem. The courses we were going to take and the precision of the sequence of events was going to have to be computed with an accuracy far beyond that demanded by ordinary circumstance.

Jacks was shaking his head all the time I was explaining it to him. But he wasn't an out and out pessimist. He had never heard of Titus Charlot, but he had the usual quasi-superstitious regard for the miracles which New Alexandria was capable of supplying to its customers. He knew he could do his part and if the rest of it couldn't be done . . . well, his ship would be restored to health for free and he was still in work.

It was a healthy attitude. I was pleased to see it. I'd encountered one or two spacemen since I came back from my involuntary exile that I wouldn't have trusted to push a pram. (Not, I hasten to add, that a liner-jockey or a company ferryman was ever called upon to do anything more complicated than pushing a pram. But somebody has to chart their perfect courses and build their spaceports for them.)

Once we'd got the matter of drawing the line between the impossible and the barely credible over and done with, Jacks naturally felt free to indulge his curiosity and ask how the hell the silly situation had arisen. I found myself somewhat at a loss to explain. I didn't want to spread nasty rumors about Gallacellan fighting ships. In the end, I wrote the whole thing off to Maslax and insanity. Ludicrous as it may seem, I felt a twinge of guilt about doing so. I wasn't wasting any sympathy for Maslax, but to write off all his actions to madness, period, seemed a little harsh. He did have a motive, when all was said and done, and his grievances were probably real. Whether he could read minds or not, there was no doubt that what he read had a touch of truth about it.

But Maslax was the only scapegoat, and Maslax was the one who was going to have to answer for it all. So I blamed it all on Maslax and madness.

Jacks was satisfied. It convinced him. I suspect that he was an easily-satisfied man.

Before we lifted I had a few words with Eve. She hadn't been present while I was exchanging unpleasantries with Charlot. She probably still thought that I was going to rescue the other half of our ill-matched crew out of sheer courage and devotion to duty. But then, she would have probably thought that anyway, and in my heart of hearts I couldn't deny a certain sense of loyalty.

"What did you tell Charlot?" she asked.

"Not a damn thing," I told her.

"You intend to keep it a big secret?" she said. "About speaking Gallacellan?"

"I don't intend telling anyone," I said. "Do you?"

She didn't answer the question. "I don't see why you want to keep quiet about it," she said. "Why do you always want to keep what you know to yourself? Charlot is desperate to contact these people. You can do it. Just like that. We don't need to do them any favors, pay them any bribes. You swore you'd never try to land on Mormyr again, after the first time. If you'd told Charlot then what you knew about the Gallacellans, and that you could speak their language, you probably wouldn't have *had* to try again. I just don't see your logic."

There was no use at all trying to explain. Not to Eve, certainly not to Charlot. There was a basic difference of opinion. Charlot wanted to talk to everybody, thought he ought to be able to, and thought he would. I don't. I don't want to, think we ought to, or think we ever will. I think the whole reason we're heading for a war is because everyone wants to own the universe, in his or her own little way. Caradoc, Charlot, the lot. They all have delusions of grandeur.

The Gallacellans didn't want to talk to me, and that was OK by me. I hadn't anything in particular to say to them. I wasn't about to do great things for the human race by becoming ambassador to the Gallacellan people any more than I was going to smash the whole Caradoc operation single-handed and save the galaxy from tragedy. Things like that just can't be done. Not now, not ever.

"Are you going to keep quite?" I asked her. "Let me get away. Let this whole matter die. Let us all write an end to this whole sick business. Are you?"

"I won't say a word," she said. She had a sense of loyalty too.

16

It is rumored that the human animal is born afraid of just two things: sudden loud noises and sudden loss of support. If that is really the case then the worst nightmare of the womb would probably simulate the experience of being jettisoned from a ship in an unpowered life raft, into the storm of Mormyr.

I didn't hit the release—the ship's computer had been entrusted with the delicate task of sending me on my way. Charlot wasn't a man to trust human reflexes where mechanical ones were available. I was in the cradle of the raft—and this was a *real* cradle, not the sort I was used to—stretched almost supine, just waiting, for long hours while the *Coregon* crawled her weary way to Mormyr and made a long, long sequence of maneuvers in order to find the very narrow groove which Jacks and Charlot had plotted between them. Nobody counted me down—there was just a voice in my ear absently remarking that we were on our way, and then more silence, total silence, until I was catapulted clear.

There was one giddy moment when I was out of the ship's g-field but still free of Mormyr's, and into that same suspended moment came the furious, hammering attack of the storm. The embryonic nightmare. I felt my heart jump, and there was a sharp pain as if a wasp had sunk its sting into the cardiac wall. The pain that came from the sudden shock of fear was a surprise to me, and I think it helped me overcome the shock, rebalancing my mind. I couldn't afford the luxury of shock—the next release was manual, and it had to be spot on. No fumbling.

I heard Jacks murmur "Good luck," and then I heard a click as he took himself out of the circuit. With the incredible clatter of the hailstones and the thunder and the buffeting wind all around me, I was suddenly aware of a complete inner silence—an utter loneliness, and seconds passed while I feared that it might stay that way, that I was deserted. Seconds of falling—free falling. I was already tensing myself for an impact that I knew was minutes away, that I knew I would not feel, because by then I would have kicked myself clear of the doomed raft.

Then Titus Charlot's voice cut in, cool and clear.

"Can you hear me, Grainger?"

"I hear you."

"Everything fine?"

A rhetorical question. Neither he nor I could know. He was working to a set of calculations on an analogue simulation. I was a prisoner inside a falling tin can. If anything was wrong, neither of us could know.

"Count," I said, feeling as if I ought to scream. There was no time for calm words—I wanted to know where I was, or rather *when*. I wanted to be into the descending chain of numbers that I knew so well. He had all the time in the world for reassuring comments and patience while he played with his simulation. Not me. These seconds might well be my last. The very least he could do was label them for me, one by one, give me something to latch on to. I was in pitch-darkness, my body weighing tons inside the armored suit, breathing bottled air, with my ears assaulted by the howling of the atmospheric chaos. I needed something to orient myself, something that pretended to have a semblance of reality. To Titus Charlot, they might only be numbers, but to me they were fragments of the real world.

He was counting. Coldly and mechanically.

I have been listening to countdowns all my life. In space—the times that I really feel alive—time revolves around countdowns. They take you beyond the light-speed on which the fabric of the universe is built, and they bring you back again. All seconds are similar, all voices are flat and unemotional. I knew Lapthorn's countdown, and Rothgar's, and Johnny's. I don't even know how I could tell them apart, but they all had some hint of individuality which marked them. Charlot's too. I had never heard a man sound so much like a clock as Charlot did. His was the absolute countdown. Pure mechanism. Perfect.

My hand gripped the release, and I knew I was squeezing. I couldn't stop. My hand was frozen to the lever like the grip of a dead man. The muscles were hard, sealed. I could feel pain in the rigidly held joints. But I couldn't relax the grip.

I was dreaming in flashes. Fully awake, but subject to ideas flitting through my mind as visual images. I dreamed that the lever jammed. I dreamed that my whole body was tight-frozen and that the count reached zero without my having pulled the release. I dreamed that the raft hit and exploded while the count was still descending, and I dreamed that my body was ripped apart in the crash, fragmenting in perfect time with the descent of the last few seconds.

All the dreams fitted into the interstices between the numbers that rolled so deadly off Charlot's distant tongue. I could imagine him sitting rock-steady at his desk, eyes glued to the simulator, his mind chasing the calculations damn near as fast as the computer, his voice mesmerized by his commitment to and involvement with the programmed flight-path of the raft. We were the same, both frozen, both living through the numbers. The only difference was that he was living the simulation, and we *knew* that would be successful. Computers don't argue. Satisfaction guaranteed. I was living the real thing, with a real life hanging on a theoretical error. I could die, while he was still counting out the measure of his computed success.

He couldn't lose.

"Twenty," he was saying, "nineteen . . ."

I needed a shot. I was dreaming I needed a shot. What I really needed was not to be so all alone. I needed to know that the shot was waiting just around the corner, that the shot was attached to a hand, that the hand was attached to Eve. I needed to know that the numbers were coming from a human voice and not from a machine. I needed to know that there was something else in the universe beside me—*beside* me. *Alongside*.

The wind didn't say a word, but he let me feel him. How? I don't know. He shuffled his feet or cracked his knuckles—something impossible, quite intangible. But enough.

Titus reached twelve, and he coughed. It was a good cough—a beautifully controlled cough. It knocked the first "e" off "eleven," and joined the count with unhurried enthusiasm. I was grateful for that cough. I was grateful for Charlot's age and poverty of health. I was grateful that my remote control wasn't as remote as it might have been.

"Ten," said Titus.

The sound of the deep, deep storm was fading in my ears. It should have been growing—the wind howling faster and harder, the lighning caging me, the hail raining down on me. But it was fading. All sound was fading. I was retreating from my senses. But Titus was still coming through. Not loud, not even clear, but *measured*. Tick, tick, tick . . .

"Four," ticked away, "three,

two,

one . . ."

Zero, and I pulled the lever.

I never heard the zero. As soon as I had located it, as soon as I knew just *when* it was, in the time-space of my seclusion, I went to it myself. I found it, on my own (though I never would have, without pointers), and I pulled the lever dead on time.

And there it was again—the sudden loss of support in a

moment of suspension and vertigo, the sudden renaissance of the storm just inches and fractions of inches away from me battering and howling like all the devils in hell at my implacable armor—nightmare. Still dreaming, still flashing across my mind in tiny packets of sensory energy. Quantum dreams, quantum nightmares.

There was light too, now. Colored light, dimmed by the smokiness of the thin transparency that served as a visor. It was four inches wide and an inch deep. No peripheral vision. No safety margin, on a heavy-duty suit. Nothing to see, except chaotic light, colored clouds lit by inconstant lightning.

Whirling. The colors whirled of their own volition, but I was turning too, turning in flight as I righted, as the power of the suit came into operation, holding me tight in arms of force, secure from harm, like bird's wings, fluttered belatedly into action to arrest a fall, to snatch a thin body back from disaster, and land . . .

Safely.

There was a soft crunch as I came to ground. I felt its softness reverberate up through my bones, as the brittle power of impact was soothed by the suit into a gentle multiple wave.

I heard nothing of the fate of the life raft. I didn't know which way it had gone. I saw nothing. Once I was free of it, it disappeared from my life. I went my own way, and landed my own way.

I landed on my feet, like a cat. I seemed to have nine lives, like a cat. Once more into hell. A cat in hell's chance. But I was still winning. Cats have a way of surviving.

Only curiosity kills cats.

There was a silence. An utter silence.

"I'm down," I said, in the fond hope that somewhere out *there* was someone who might be interested to know.

I heard Titus Charlot. He wasn't answering—he was breathing. His mouth must have been very close to the microphone. I had the odd idea that I was hearing Titus Charlot, speechless. An unusual experience.

"Stay still," he said, eventually. "I'm hooking the *Hooded Swan* back into the circuit."

"What about Jacks?" I said, with commendable concern for the good of my fellow man. "Did he get the ship out all right?"

"We'll know in a moment," said Charlot. "He's still in atmosphere. I'll let him in for a moment, as soon as we know he's clear. But only a moment. We have no time to waste."

No, I thought. We never have.

For just the moment that Charlot promised, the circuit was connected four ways.

"I'm down," I said again.

There was a crackle as Nick delArco said something both thankful and crude, while Jacks expressed his surprise and pleasure in like manner. Neither was talking to me, and the microphones failed to make their words clear. The meaning, however, was successfully conveyed.

"I'm a rich man," said Jacks, just a second or two later. "Just don't make any mistakes lifting that baby."

I didn't have to ask whether his part had come off all right. I could practically hear him counting his money. He was in clean space.

He cut out of the circuit.

"Right," said Charlot. "Now we have to find out how far away you are and guide you in. Switch on your bleep."

I substituted the signal for the sound of my voice, and I waited. I couldn't hear what was going on, but I could imagine it well enough. Titus was telling Nick how to use the ship's sensors to fix the bleep. I gave them a good two minutes and switched myself back on.

"Where am I?" I said.

"Impatient," said Nick. "Keep bleeping."

I gave him another two minutes.

"How far?" I asked, just to vary the dialogue.

"Spot on," he said. "Less than twenty miles."

Mormyr is a big world, and she blows big winds. Twenty miles was, indeed, spot on. But we needed that accuracy. On full power, the suit could take me three, maybe four miles an hour. And depending on how much power had gone up the chute making sure I landed properly, I probably had no more than eight hours in hand. Twenty miles was a real bull's-eye, and if it had been a competition we'd have won. But at the time, I could only feel that we'd brought it off according to plan, that we'd scraped home by a short head.

I still had those miles to walk.

It took me more than four hours, and it was very boring. I've walked the surfaces of some very strange worlds in my time—and some rather violent ones too. But for sheer hostility there was nothing to approach Mormyr. In a way, that long walk was a privileged experience. But I'm not one for telling barroom tales, and I have no grandchildren. I measure experiences by what they are— not what they'll add to me in years to come. That twenty miles in the kaleidoscopic tempest was just twenty very uncomfortable miles. There was nothing much to look at—two minutes of chaos is quite enough to provide a lifetime's memory.

The walking wasn't particularly hard—the suit provided the power to move itself and some of the power to move me—but it was by no means easy. I was totally unused to the type of suit, and after a few minutes I found it increasingly difficult to keep in step with it. It rubbed me at several points—particularly around my waist and in my legs, and it grew progressively more painful. I began the trek with light conversation—mostly directed at Nick and Johnny but long before I was halfway I had degenerated to complaints—mostly directed at Charlot and providence— and simple but ingenious curses.

Nick volunteered to come and meet me, but I told him not to be a damned fool. We had no suit as heavy as mine on the *Swan* and he'd have been taking a hell of a risk coming out in something that the hailstones wouldn't just bounce off.

I think the worst of the walk was that it interfered so much with the harsh beauty of the operation. If it had simply been a matter of that heartrending drop, followed by a smooth takeoff and return to safety, the whole rescue would have had a kind of elegance, even to my crude and matter-of-fact aesthetic sensibilities. But that walk destroyed all the fine feeling and triumph that I might have derived from the affair. By the time I reached the *Swan* I ached, I was sore, and I was in a thoroughly bad mood. Right back into the old Grainger groove. Without that long walk, I could almost have *felt* like a hero. I could have kidded myself, for a while at least. But there is something about having the insides of your thighs rubbed red raw that restores a somewhat callous persepctive on life. There is something noble and heroic about a trickle of blood from the corner of one's mouth, or a discreetly bloody wound. There is nothing subtly uplifting about a sore bum.

The welcome I got from Captain delArco was almost sufficient to restore my faith in heroic nature. He was just perfect. He was a big man with a deep voice, and never given to leaping about with lunatic enthusiasm, so he playe1 the part with wonderful self-control. But every time I moved I reminded myself of the true facts of life, and I was able to play *my* part down to the last grunt and scowl. Nick had spent a lot of time being resentful of that grunt and scowl in the past, but at that moment he began to love them in spite of themselves. As for Johnny—well, I think Johnny had always had perfect faith in the fact that I would come knocking on the door to pull him out of the jaws of death. I was only living up to his expectations.

Between the two of them, they worked their way into the depths of the suit and pulled me out of it. They had to hold me up for a while so that proper circulation could be restored to my system. Then I went away and was unreasonably extravagant with the ship's water supply by having a hot bath. There is, I admit, a ludicrous quality about taking time out for a bath in the middle of a rescue operation, but I really did not feel competent to lift the ship until I had soothed my more tender parts. I had every confidence in the ship's anchors, and I thought that staying put for an extra half hour was less hazardous than lifting while I was in less-than-fit condition.

When I was good and ready, I put on clean clothes, had a cup of coffee, and went back to the control room. Johnny was already nursing the drive into a state of readiness. Nick took up a position beside me, ready with the needle, and I told him which shot to use, how much and when.

"OK, Titus," I said without preamble, knowing that he would still be waiting at the call-circuit. "You can sign the check now. I'm bringing your bird back."

Then I took off.

17

I honestly thought that was the end. I thought that it finished Titus Charlot, finished the *Hooded Swan,* finished delArco and Lapthorn's sister and Herault's grandson. I thought that I had placed a full stop at the end of a chapter in my life.

If anything, of course, it would have been a beginning rather than an end. It would have been the beginning of a new career as a space-tramp, and a dead-ender. I wasn't afraid of such a career. I knew it was the way of all flesh. That was what I expected. But I was thinking "out" rather than "in." I was thinking of all the nasty things I was getting well out of rather than all the nasty things I was heading for. I wasn't blind—I'd made a real choice—and I thought I'd made the right decision.

I was simply wrong. I just couldn't put an end to it. I'd overestimated myself. I don't mean, of course, that I went back to Charlot and told him to burn his check because I couldn't bear to part. I quit all right. I quit, I cleared my debt, and I went away—shipped out from Iniomi to Pallant and from Pallant just as soon and as far as I could go. I wrote an end to the story

But the threads of the plot always go on beyond the end of the story. There is never any real ending. I couldn't put an end to the plot The threads were still

going on, and they were still attached to me. There was no
way out of the plot at all.

It was going to catch up with me again.

Someday.

CAP KENNEDY . . .

If you loved Star Trek, if you find Doc Savage not sf enough, if action-space adventure is your dish, then this all-new interstellar series is your guarantee of great space fiction!